MONEY IN THE GRAVE 2

Lock Down Publications and Ca$h Presents

MONEY IN THE GRAVE 2

A Novel by *Martell "Troublesome" Bolden*

Lock Down Publications

Po Box 944
Stockbridge, Ga 30281

Visit our website @
www.lockdownpublications.com

Lock Down Publications
Like our page on Facebook: Lock Down Publications @
www.facebook.com/lockdownpublications.ldp

Book interior design by: **Shawn Walker**
Edited by: **Shamika Smith**

Stay Connected with Us!

Text **LOCKDOWN** to 22828 to stay up-to-date with new releases, sneak peaks, contests and more...
Thank you.

Submission Guideline.

Submit the first three chapters of your completed manuscript to ldpsubmissions@gmail.com, subject line: Your book's title. The manuscript must be in a .doc file and sent as an attachment. Document should be in Times New Roman, double spaced and in size 12 font. Also, provide your synopsis and full contact information. If sending multiple submissions, they must each be in a separate email.

Have a story but no way to send it electronically? You can still submit to LDP/Ca$h Presents. Send in the first three chapters, written or typed, of your completed manuscript to:

LDP: Submissions Dept
Po Box 944
Stockbridge, Ga 30281

DO NOT send original manuscript. Must be a duplicate.

Provide your synopsis and a cover letter containing your full contact information.

Thanks for considering LDP and Ca$h Presents.

In memory of my beloved mother, Ethel "Momma" Miller. Sunrise: December 15th, 1940 - Sunset: September 19th, 2021

Momma, there's no way for me to ever love you more than you loved me. No matter my wrong choices in life, I could never do any wrong in your eyes. Without you, I wouldn't be the man that I stand to be. You raised me and many others to the best of your ability. I appreciate all of your sacrifices and efforts to make sure we had all that we needed. You gave us holidays and other special occasions with just the little that you had, just to show us how much you loved us. I will never forget the childhood memories of you being there for me ever since I could remember. You were the soul of our family, and now, may your soul rest in power. I will forever miss you. Though you are gone, you will never be forgotten. Momma, until we meet again, I will be looking for your face in the sky...

~Your loving son

Martell "Troublesome" Bolden

CHAPTER 1

I can't believe what the fuck happened to Don. Someone had to have him set up, Rich contemplated. He blamed himself for his brother being robbed and killed last night, and finding out who was responsible was his motive so he could make him pay in blood.

Once the elevator dinged open onto the sixth-floor corridor of St. Joseph's Hospital, Rich stepped out. He headed for room 414. Approaching the room, Rich reached for its handle, and the door was pulled open by a short, petite, brown complexioned nurse, who accidentally bumped into him as she exited.

"This is Shanta Henderson's room," Rich said more than inquired.

The nurse nodded. "Yes, it is."

"How is she?" He dreaded the answer, not knowing what to expect.

"She suffered a flesh wound. Other than being in need of some rest, she'll be just fine." The nurse offered him a smile before waltzing away.

Rich entered the room and quietly closed the door behind himself. He found Shanta lying awake in bed, peering out of the window at the early morning sky. She had a bag of blood under pressure dripping into a line in her arm and a large white bandage covering her upper left chest that was stained pink from her superficial bullet wound. Seeing her like that, he immediately grew even more enraged with whoever did this to her and Don, and he hoped that she may be able to assist him in finding them.

Rich stepped over to her bedside and said, "Shanta, I still can't believe what happened to you and Don."

"I'm sorry about your brother, Rich. Really, I am," Shanta wept. She sat up in bed with the help of Rich.

"Did you see the niggas responsible?" he eagerly wanted to know.

"N-no... They were wearing masks. All I remember is being shot before losing consciousness."

Rich gripped her arm and demanded, "Are you sure you didn't see any of the niggas?!"

"Rich, don't you think if I did see any of them, then I would surely tell you! I love Don and would do anything to help you get the niggas who killed him, not to mention they nearly killed me too!" she cried.

Regaining his composure, Rich let go of her arm. "I know, Shan. I just want them niggas to pay in blood for what they did to you and my bro. At least you're still alive." He noticed Shanta hang her head. "What's the matter?"

"I... I was pregnant. Due to going into shock, I had a miscarriage," she said in a lowered voice as tears wet her cheeks. It was hard on her losing Don and even harder that she lost their unborn child.

"Did Don know about the pregnancy?"

"No, he didn't. I had just found out myself and planned to tell him about it during the next Sunday dinner at your mother's."

Rich rubbed her back in solace and said, "Sorry that you lost the baby, Shan. I'm sure it's hard on you even more than it'll be on mama." He knew their mom yearned for either Don or himself to give her a grandchild, and now that was taken away.

"How is Angie after all?" Shanta wanted to know.

"She's tryin' to hold it together. I just hope losin' Don doesn't cause her to backslide after all he did to help her get clean."

"Well, I hope she'll be fine." Shanta peered away out the window and said, "Now that I've lost Don and his baby, I'll never have a piece of him in my life."

"You still have me. And I know how much Don loved you, so I'll always be here for you on the strength of him."

She brought her eyes to Rich's. "That means so much to me," she told him and then pulled him in for a much-needed hug.

At that moment, the door came open, and in came Parker along with Kat. They came bearing "Get Well" balloons and teddy bears from the hospital's gift shop. After receiving a call about what had happened to their girl, Parker and Kat wanted to be there for Shanta. They knew she needed their love now more than ever. Both girls hurried over to Shan's bedside, happy to see her alive, and nearly hugged her to death.

"Shan, we were so worried about you," Parker said, sounding concerned yet relieved.

"Yes, girl. We're glad that you're alright," Kat added.

"I'll live. But Don..." Shanta's words trailed off.

Parker sat on the edge of the bed and grabbed Shanta's hand in hers. "It's so sad what happened to Don. He was a good nigga."

"And you deserved the love and happiness he brought you," Kat input.

"I... I also lost our baby," Shanta found it hard to say aloud as tears streamed her cheeks.

"OMG!" Parker gasped.

"Why didn't you tell us that you were pregnant, Shan?" Kat asked curiously.

"I just wanted to tell Don first, but I never got the chance to," Shanta answered in close to a whisper.

Rich couldn't stand to hear more, so he decided to leave Shanta with her friends. "Listen, Shan. I'll leave you with your homegirls. If you need me for anything, then just give me a call," he told her.

"Okay, Rich. I'll be sure to call."

Parker turned to Rich and voiced, "I'm sorry about Don."

"So am I," Kat included. "Don shouldn't have died in vain."

"And I'll make sure his death is honored," Rich vowed. With no further words, he turned on his way out of the room, vowing to avenge Don as his brother's keeper.

•••

Rob, TJ, Max, and Bone were gathered in the hotel room of the seedy Diamond Inn where they were to divide the cash four ways which they had come up on from the lick on Don. Rob stood peering out the window into the dark pink sky while TJ paced the floor lost in thought, and Bone and Max sat at the worn table handling the paper.

After robbing and killing Don for his goods, the gang had gone and sold the three blocks they'd collected to Heavy and Swindle for the low. Shit had gone exactly as Swindle and Bone schemed it up, unbeknownst to any of the others. And Bone wanted to keep it that way.

The major lick Rob still had lined up was on his mind. He knew it could be the biggest one they'd hit yet. And he also knew it would take some precise planning to pull it off. However, Rob was confident that he and his gang could get it done. He turned towards the others and told them: "I got a big lick lined up. One that could set us all straight."

"How big you talkin'?" Bone wanted to know, peering up at him.

"Bigger than any licks we hit before."

Max looked up from dividing the money and asked, "Who's the nigga, and when do we lay his ass down?"

"Still figurin' that out as of now, but just know it's in the works," Rob assured.

TJ stopped in his tracks. "After this, what's next?" he asked no one in particular, looking around the room at each of his boys.

"We enjoy this cash, that's what," Max said as he counted out a stack of twenties.

"Don't y'all niggas want more outta life than just some damn cash?"

Max snorted. "I'ont know about you, but cash rules everything around me."

Stepping over to the table, where there were four piles of money along with four poles, TJ grabbed a fistful of the loose bills and stated, "And when all of this shit is gone, then what? Huh? 'Cause money comes and goes." He tossed the bills back on the table with the rest.

"Then we do what we've always done and hit another lick," Bone piped in assertively.

"Straight up. It's what we do," Max agreed.

"From the sounds of it, all you niggas plan to do is hit licks for the rest of y'all lives. Well, not me."

The room grew silent as the others took a moment to take in what TJ had announced. After all, he had been through with the gang, TJ knew this would be the final time they would be together like this. He didn't know exactly how the others would react to him deciding to get out of the stick-up game. However, he figured while they were all together and amongst themselves, it was the best time to let them know. TJ wondered if any of the others ever thought about getting out of the game also. If they were smart, then they would get out before it's too late, is how he thought.

Breaking the silence, Max raved, "Fuck you mean by that?"

"I mean, I'm done with hittin' licks," TJ affirmed.

"Dis nigga can't be fuckin' serious right now!" Bone said disapprovingly.

"I am as serious as it gets."

Bone snorted. "Can't believe this shit. After all of the robbin' and killin' we've done together, suddenly you have a change of fuckin' heart." Given that he himself was a heartless goon, he definitely wasn't feelin' the shit.

"TJ, we're s'posed to be gang," Max protested.

"And we are gang. This doesn't change that. Look, I'ont expect either of you to agree with my decision. Although, I do expect for you to respect it."

"We can, and we will respect your decision, TJ," Rob assured, speaking on his and the others' behalfs. "All I ask is that you stay down until after the big lick I have in line. I'm sure we'll need your gun. Besides, then you'll be able to walk away with more cash than you ever had at once."

"Let his ass be done. Just means more money for us," Bone remarked.

"Bone, no matter what, he's our nigga," Max told him.

"How 'bout it, TJ? Are you down for one final lick?" Rob wanted to know.

"I'm down. But after the lick, I'm done for good," TJ swore.

Rob nodded. "Then it's settled, and you're right. Maybe we should all think about changin' the game."

"Understand somethin'; the game don't change. Just the players do," Bone remarked. He resumed dividing the cash.

The entire gang sat at the table in silence as the dividends were handed out, following dividing the cash that they each ended up with 40Gs. It wasn't much, although it was enough. Rob knew they had to pull off a much bigger caper in order for him to reach his goal soon. With the money he had buried in the grave already, he just needed a few hundred Gs more, and he hoped the next mark he had in line would bring him that.

While the others were satisfied with their take, Bone expected there to be more. "Can't fuckin' believe this is all the paper we got outta this shit," he commented heatedly.

"Good thing there's always more where this comes from," Rob input, thumbing through a stack of dead presidents.

"Rob already has a major lick on deck for us," Max added.

"And there would be more money in it for us without this nigga." Bone cut his eyes at TJ. "So, if he wants to be done, then let it be," he growled.

Leaning forward and resting his elbows on the table, TJ glared over at Bone and told him, "Let's get one thing straight. The only reason I even decided to hit the lick is because Rob wants me to. Unlike you, I'm not hurtin' for money."

Bone jumped to his feet abruptly, knocking over his chair. "Recognize who the fuck you talkin' to, TJ!" he raged.

TJ leaned back in his chair, undisturbed. He eyed Bone narrowly and stated, "Real only recognize real, right?" His tone was smooth, yet his eyes were sharp.

"Enough with the beef," Rob spoke up. "Besides Bone, you can't feel some typa way towards TJ for decidin' to do what's best for him."

"This between me and TJ right now. Why don't you stay outta it?" Bone remarked.

Feeling like his gangsta was being tested, TJ sniped, "Don't get it wrong, my G is official."

Bone glared at TJ and then cut his eyes to his Glock .19 lying atop the table along with the others' poles. He was tempted to go for his. Taking notice, TJ candidly placed a hand on his own .40 caliber as he grimaced at Bone. Both niggas held each other's eyes without wavering. It had become a hostile situation.

"TJ, Bone, enough." Rob intervened before shit went too far. He stood and began making his way around the table. "Look at us. We're better than this. After all the shit we been through and niggas we had to tend to, there should be no reason any of us to turn on each other now." Stepping over to Bone, he suggested, "This ain't for us. Let bygones be bygones."

"Yeah, whateva," Bone replied pugnaciously. He grabbed up his pole and placed it on his waist, then began stuffing his take of the cash into the pockets of his Blue Bands Only jeans, not caring to hear shit. Afterwards, he headed for the room's door.

"Don't just walk out on us, Bone," Max called after him.

Bone peered back over his shoulder and stated, "Tell that shit to TJ. He's the one walkin' out." He exited the room and slammed the door shut behind himself.

Rob placed a hand on Max's shoulder, halting him from going after Bone. "Let him go. He needs time to clear his mind. We all do." He understood that a goon with money on his mind more than likely had his mind on murder.

CHAPTER 2

Overhead, the sky was filled with gray rainclouds, fitting the gloomy moment. The burial grounds were surrounded by those close to Don. Everyone was dressed in black suits and dresses. As the black casket with gold trim was lowered into the grave, Rich watched with a heavy heart. Angie quietly wept into her tissue. Shanta cried as she reminisced about all of the times she had shared with Don. And T-Mac, C-note, and Danger silently paid their respects as Don was laid to rest. The death of Don was hard on all of them in one way or another.

Rich embraced his mom. "Ma, just know that I'm here for you as much as Don was," he told her.

"I know. Richard, I realize that your brother meant so much to you. He practically raised you when I wasn't around to do so myself. And, believe me, I'm hurting too. So, I need you to be strong for me," Angie consoled.

"Ma, I just wish that I woulda been there for him, then maybe things woulda been different."

"Then maybe it woulda been you who lost your life instead. Have you ever thought about that? So maybe it's a good thing you weren't there," she reasoned.

Rich found her eyes and stated, "No matter what, I'm willin' to ride or die for Don."

"And I respect that. I just don't want you dying when you don't have to. Donte wouldn't want that for you either."

"What he'd want is for me to avenge him. He'd do that for me." Rage rose within him.

"Baby, I just don't want you to die with a vengeance. I already loss Don and I don't want to lose you too, Rich," Angie expressed.

"Listen, Ma. At least if I do die, then it won't be in vain," Rich declared. He wouldn't let anything or none prevent him from avenging the death of his brother, and Angie knew that.

Angie rubbed his cheek and said, "Don's fortunate to have a brother in you. Look, I'll see you back at home for the commemoration." She pecked his cheek before heading for the car.

Rich told Brittany to ride home with his mom while he sticks around. He then stepped over to Shanta, who was bawling. Given the fact that she not only lost Don, but also their unborn child made it all tougher on her. Rich knew she was hurting more than himself, which enraged him further and caused him to want the niggas responsible for the pain.

"Shan," Rich began gingerly. "I know it won't bring back Don nor the baby, but I'm here for you."

"What am I supposed to do without him? He and I were supposed to spend the rest of our lives together." Tears caused Shanta's mascara to trek down her cheeks.

"You're supposed to go on with livin' your life, Shan. It's what Don would want for you. I know it's not easy, but it's best."

"And what about you? I'm sure losing Don isn't easy for you either."

"No, it isn't. But gettin' the niggas who took him away from us will ease my pain." Rich's tone was solemn.

"Rich, I want for you to get whomever the niggas are just as bad. And I'm down to do anything I can for Don, no matter what," she vowed.

Rich smirked. "Don always said that you're a down ass bitch. Just make sure you take care of yourself."

"Just know that I'll always love Don."

"I know you will."

Shanta's girls, Parker and Kat, were awaiting her. "Rich, I'll see you at the gathering back at your mom's place." She gave him a hug before turning on her way.

Thunder rumbled in the distance while Rich stood, taking one final look at Don's casket as a single tear slid down his face. T-Mac stepped up beside his cousin and placed a hand on Rich's shoulder in solace.

C-note and Danger made their way over beside Rich and T-Mac. The four of them had served as pall bearers during the funeral ceremony. Now seeing Don's casket in the grave made his death all too real. They all knew that Don would be knee-deep in the game until the casket dropped. Rain began to sprinkle, and thunder cracked. Rich, T-Mac, C-note, and Danger were the last ones remaining at the gravesite. As rain fell on them, they each stood there, giving Don a moment of silence.

"Your moms told me that you were over here grievin' over your bro. Listen, I'm fucked up behind Don bein' murked too," T-Mac expressed.

"Then let's make sure we get the niggas responsible for murkin' him," Rich asserted.

"You know I'm down."

"First, we gotta find them niggas," C-note piped in.

"And I won't stop til I do," Rich assured.

"Can't let them niggas get away with that shit," Danger added.

"That's why I need you and T-Mac in the streets handlin' beef while me and C-note handle the money."

"On it," T-Mac said. "I'm still lookin' to handle the beef after niggas popped me any-fuckin'-way."

"This may be too soon, but," C-note spoke up, "there's still money to be made."

"But without Don, we don't have a plug," Danger said.

"Leave it to me because I already know someone who we can plug in with that I'll be sure to discuss business with," Rich replied.

"We'll need at least three birds to keep up with the demand," C-note told him.

"I'll see what I can come up with. Look, since Don's gone, I'll be bossin' up, and I expect to keep shit together," Rich told the gang.

C-note placed a hand on Rich's shoulder. "You know, bein' a boss ain't as easy as Don made it look. So, if you're gonna assume the position, then you gotta move like a boss. Your big bro was my nigga, and I was down for him without a doubt. And outta respect for him, I'm down for you too."

"Same," Danger added.

"And you already know I'm down for you, cuz," T-Mac input.

"Only thing is, I need niggas to respect my position regardless of my brother bein' Don," Rich stressed. He knew the streets respected Don, although Rich didn't want to live in the shadow of his brother. He was out to gain his own respect, even if he had to demand it.

"Rich, riches, and savages are the only things niggas respect in these streets," C-note gamed him.

Rich looked out at the rainclouds and stated, "Then I'ma show these niggas in the streets that I'm a rich savage."

"Let's just keep our heads up and only down when we pray," C-note said.

Removing the Glock .45 from his waist, Rich cocked back its slide until he ejected every bullet from the thirty-shot clip, which dropped into Don's grave. He then declared, "Bullets over prayers."

CHAPTER 3

Ever since hitting the lick on Don, the gang hadn't hung out much. So tonight, Rob wanted them to meet up to have some drinks and chill. In the pool hall, Rob, TJ, and Bone stood around a pool table while awaiting the arrival of Max. Something that bothered Rob was all of the flexin' Max had been doing on Instagram lately because Rob knew it was best for a jack-boy to keep a low profile. He definitely didn't want to raise any suspicions.

"So, Rob, what's up with the major lick you have lined up? Any new details?" Bone wanted to know.

Rob took a swig from his glass of Henny. "As soon as I know, then so will you," he responded. "But check it out. I ain't here to discuss licks. I'm here to chill with you, TJ, and Max."

"Speakin' of, Max shoulda been here almost an hour ago," TJ commented, glancing at his Patek.

"Don't trip. He'll be here soon," Bone assured.

"Max ass has been doin' the most lately, and I ain't feelin' that shit. He shouldn't be coppin' all of the fuckin' jewels and whips and shit," Rob complained.

Bone chalked the tip of his pool stick. "Max is just enjoyin' his paper, and I'ont see anything wrong with that." He lined up the pool stick then took a shot at the billiards.

"What's wrong with it is he's doin' it for the 'Gram."

"His last post is too hard," TJ input, referring to Max posting on Instagram a picture of himself rocking a ski mask while sitting on the couch with stacks of cash on the coffee table along with an AR-15, which he captioned: #DawnOfANewDon.

At that moment, Max entered the poolhall. He was drippin' in ice on his neck and both wrists. Noticing the gang, he stepped over to where they were. He and Bone dapped.

"Max, I can't believe you're splurgin' on ice, and shit like the money is legit. We're jack-boys, so we need to keep a low profile," Rob told him angrily.

"We jack niggas for their money in order to spend. Money comes and goes; then we hit another lick," Max reasoned.

TJ scoffed. "You just don't seem to get it, Max."

"Stay outta this, TJ, because this has nothin' to do with you," Max sniped.

"This has somethin' to do with all of us when Max is puttin' us in jeopardy," remarked TJ.

"I don't give a fuck how you feel, TJ!" Max spat.

Rob grabbed Max by the shirt and stated, "Nigga, don't forget who has your fuckin' back, a'ight."

"Chill the fuck out, Rob." Bone shoved Rob away from Max. "Now is not the time for this shit."

"Bone's right," TJ added.

Rob eyed Max and said, "You really don't get it, Max." He turned for the exit with TJ on his heels.

"What I'ont get is you," Max barked behind Rob as he made his way out the poolhall. Max was stressed. "I need a fuckin' drink."

"Then why don't we hit up the bar." Bone led the way over to the bar, where they took up two vacant stools. He ordered himself a bottle of Budweiser while Max ordered a double shot of Remy. Bone took a swig of his beer then said, "Listen, don't let that shit with Rob bother you. He just expects us all to be like him. Well, Rob can leave that to TJ. Maybe we'll be better off without them." Bone figured now was a better time than any to plant a seed.

"Yeah, maybe. But I have no doubt that Rob and TJ are still down for us."

"If you say so." Bone took a swig of his beer. He noticed Benny enter the poolhall. "I'll be back in a sec," Bone said before making his way over to Benny.

Benny was lining up a shot on the pool table as he asked, "Got all of my money, Bone?"

"Count it if you want," Bone said and tossed a bankroll atop the pool table. With no further words, he then returned to the stool at the bar.

"Hell was that about?" Max wanted to know.

"Nothin'. Let's bounce." Bone drowned the remains of his beer before he and Max headed out the poolhall.

•••

It was the wee hours of the morning when Bone had peeped Benny emerge from the pool hall. Out for retribution, Bone had awaited Benny while sitting in a parked car. He wasn't willing to allow Benny's ass to get away with threatening his life over money, even though he had paid up. But now, it was his time for payback. Bone slid outta the car with his gun in hand.

After having put back some shots of liquor, Benny was apparently tipsy. He slightly staggered as he headed towards his Cadillac. Being caught off guard, Benny felt a barrel of a gun pressed to the back of his head.

"Thought I'd just let you get away with threatenin' me over some fuckin' money," Bone hissed. He searched Benny and confiscated his revolver.

"So, this how it is, Bone?" Benny replied soberly.

"It is what it is. Now get your bitch-ass in the trunk!"

Bone took Benny's keys and then forced him into the trunk of his own car. He then hopped inside the 'Lac and drove away from the pool hall on his way to someplace secluded. Shortly thereafter, Bone pulled the car inside an abandoned garage. He opened the trunk and then trained his gun down on Benny, who was scared for his life.

Benny threw his hands up in surrender. "Listen, Bone, if this is about the cash you paid me, then you can take it back," he pled.

"It's about more than just the money. I ain't with lettin' no muthafucka threaten me and live to make good on it."

"How 'bout I pay back double. Plus, you won't have to worry about me tryin' to get revenge."

Bone mean mugged him. "I ain't worried about nothin'. And you can just pay back with your life," he hissed and then successively squeezed the trigger.

Boc, boc, boc, boc, boc!

The bullets riddled Benny's chest, and Bone watched as Benny took his final breath. After taking back his money, leaving the dead body inside the trunk of the car, and before fleeing the scene, Bone set the abandoned garage aflame.

CHAPTER 4

"Ma, I'm here," Rich announced as he entered Angie's home.

He was there to check in on her to be sure that she was okay. After shutting the door behind himself, he then stepped further inside and found himself looking at the collection of childhood photos of him and Don on the mantle. Rich couldn't help but feel grief. Growing up, all the two had were each other for the most part. It was Don who had taught Rich how to ride a bike and how to ride on his enemies. And Rich would remember everything his big brother taught him in order to put the streets on lock. First thing first, he needed to make the streets feel his presence.

Angie stepped up beside him and said, "This one is my favorite." She referred to a photo of a young Don and Rich at the park dressed alike, and Don held up bunny ear fingers behind the head of a snaggletooth Rich.

"Ma, how you holdin' up after all?"

"I have my days."

"Listen," Rich moved near her, "I know you're missin' Don as much as I am. Even though he's gone, we'll never allow him to be forgotten."

"It's just there's not a day I don't feel like I should have been there much more for Don and you. Then just maybe, all would be different. I must admit that the guilt eats at me," she expressed. "What hurts me the most is that I haven't had much of a chance to be a mom to you and Don. The moment I get myself together, and I have the chance, I end up losing your brother. The hardest thing for a mother is to lose a child, no matter how old he is. And now I'll never have the chance to be the mom to Don that he deserved." Tears began sliding down Angie's cheeks. She was taking the loss of Don harder than ever and just needed to find a way to cope.

Rich looked into her teary eyes. "We already got past this. Nothing's your fault, Ma. Trust and believe that bro always felt very deservin' to have you as a mom. He's the one who always reminded me that we have to love you no matter what. Just look at all the love he showed you by helpin' you get clean and buyin' you this home. Don't that tell you just how much he loved you as a mom?"

"You're right," Angie answered through sniffles. "And I truly do appreciate all of the things that Don did for me. But what I appreciate most is him making sure me and you are close."

"And I'll always be close to you, Ma. It's what Don would want of us." Rich tightly embraced his mom.

She peered up into his eyes, which were as hard as the steel she had felt on his waist, and said, "And apparently you believe always having a gun close to you is what Don would want, too."

"Listen, Ma, after what happened to bro, I ain't bein' caught dead without it," Rich replied as a matter of fact.

"That's what I'm afraid of, Rich. You'll end up dead like your brother. I know you want whoever did this to Don."

"Not only did they kill Don, but they also shot Shanta, which resulted in her losin' she and Don's unborn child. I can't live with myself knowin' whoever did this is still alive."

"Rich, two wrongs don't make a right," Angie tried to reason.

"You're wrong, Ma. If they take a life, we take a life," was his philosophy.

"Just don't let it turn you into something that you're not."

Rich met her eyes, his hard. "Ma, what do you mean?"

"I mean, you don't have to take your brother's place."

"It's too late for that. What's his is mine. And I'll make him proud," he stated.

"I'm sure you mean by going after whoever killed him."

"For starters, yes. But overall, I mean by takin' over the streets in Don's wake."

Angie let out a sigh. "Baby, the streets don't owe you a damn thing."

"Ma, the streets owe for takin' away Don," Rich remarked. "And I'm gonna make the streets pay in blood."

"Listen, Richard," she began solemnly. "If you're gonna play the streets, then play for keeps."

"It's the only way," Rich assured. "Look, I got some things to tend to, so I have to get goin'." He pecked his mom on the cheek before heading out the front door.

Outside, Rich made his way towards his Lexus, which was parked curbside. He stepped inside and brought the engine to life before stabbing off down the street, listening to Polo G's tune "Losses."

•••

Shanta sat on the couch crying her eyes out with Parker and Kat there comforting her. She and her girls were in the condo Don had bought for them. Though it had been a couple of weeks since Don's funeral, Shan was still grieving over him. Not to mention she grieved over the loss of their unborn. It was as if she was missing pieces of her heart.

"Shan, I hate seeing you like this," Parker said. She was seated beside Shanta, rubbing her back in solace. "I can't even imagine what you're going through."

Kat came in from the kitchen with three wine glasses a bottle of Kim Crawford wine. "Don was a good nigga and all, but Shan, you need to dry your eyes and get on with your life," she said plainly.

"Kathrine!" Parker scolded her.

"What? I'm just saying. She can't let what happened stop her from living her life." Kat poured them each a nice amount of wine.

"She needs us to be here for her right now. Not tell her what we think is or isn't good for her."

"No, what she needs right now is a drink." Kat handed Shanta a glass filled nearly to its rim. "Listen, girl. There are more niggas out there like Don. Now drink up."

Shanta peered at her through tormented eyes. "Kat, this isn't about some nigga. It's about me losing Don and our baby. Sorry if I'm killing your vibe, but that's something I'll need some time to get by," she told Kat.

"Girl, I'm sorry if I seem insensitive to your losses. You know I'm here for you."

"Shan, Kat may be a lot of things, but she has always been there for you and me. We've all always been here for each other," Parker input.

"I know, and I appreciate having you two as friends," Shanta expressed.

Kat sipped at her drink. "Shan, what are you gonna do now that Don's gone?"

"What Kat means is, do you have any plans moving forward," Parker rephrased.

"All I can do is take it a day at a time as of now. I'm sure that in due time I'll be able to refocus on my life," Shanta answered.

"Take all the time you need."

"What you need is to spend some time out on the town, so we can get your mind off things," Kat suggested.

"Kat, your ass only wanna go out just so niggas can be all up in our faces. Well, Shan don't need that right now," Parker objected.

"Parker, the only reason you don't care to go out is because you got yourself a new man. The nigga must be puttin' it down on you good." Kat smirked.

"First off, Castle isn't the only reason why. And second, I'm sure Shan agrees with me."

Shanta took a sip of the wine. "Parker's right. I'm not in the mood to be out and about. Let's just chill here, and maybe we'll go out some other night." She wasn't quite ready to put herself out there because she wasn't over Don.

CHAPTER 5

Rich, along with T-Mac, was admitted into the trap spot where they were led inside the basement. Rich was there to meet with Heavy to discuss business. Now that Rich was in charge of the operations, he needed a plug in order to keep up with the supply and demand. He or none of the others were familiar with Don's plug, being that as a precaution, Castle had only dealt with Don. Therefore, it left Rich to find his own plug, and Heavy would have to do.

Heavy was shooting a game of pool with Swindle as Rich approached. A few of their goons were present, including Vito, who was tempted to bang Rich on the spot after poppin' him and smokin' his boy, Q. However, Heavy needed things to be copacetic while he raps with Rich.

"What you drinkin' on?" offered Heavy.

"Remy. Double shot," Rich requested.

"Nothin' for me," T-Mac declined the offer. He wanted to be on point while in the presence of Heavy, and especially Swindle, who he didn't trust one bit. And at some point, he would get at the nigga behind having him shot. But for now, he had to play shit cool.

"Baby girl, grab homeboy his drink," he directed the bad bitch seated at the wet bar. Returning his attention to Rich, Heavy said, "Heard about Don. He was a real one, despite our differences. Any clue who murked him?"

"None yet. However, we gon' tear the streets apart until we find out."

Swindle knocked a pool ball into the corner pocket. "And what y'all gon' do if you find out?"

"Then we gon' make the streets bleed murder," T-Mac piped in sternly. He and Swindle eyed each other intensely.

"Dig, if I find out whoever had anything to do with Don bein' murked, then you'll be the first to know," Heavy told them. On the low, Heavy didn't give a fuck about Don being murdered because it was less of a competitor he had in the game. However, he failed to realize that, in a way, he was tied into Don's murder on behalf of Swindle, who just shook his damn head at how naïve Heavy was but kept that shit to himself.

"Look, I'll focus on findin' out who murked Don. All I need you to do is plug me with some yae," Rich told him.

"A'ight. So, what can I do for you on the yae tip?"

"For starters, three keys. And if our business goes well, then I'll cop more on the re-up."

"Cool. Usually, I'd tax thirty-five Gs apiece. But outta respect for Don, I'll accept thirty," he pitched.

"Check it out, Heavy, my business with you don't have shit to do with my brother. And I'ont need your pity. But since you named the price, then it's settled," Rich remarked.

"Now that we got that understood, I'll keep our business between us."

"Sounds good. Soon as I get the cash in order, then I'll be in touch." Rich polished off his drink and then sat the glass on the edge of the pool table before turning for the exit with T-Mac in tow.

Heavy lined up his pool stick to take a shot. "Obviously, the nigga Rich is out to replace Don, and he's gonna go hard behind his murder," he commented.

"Think he has it in him to be like his brother?" Swindle inquired. He would also get Rich out the way just the same if need be.

"Naw. Rich don't know what it takes to be a boss in this game." Heavy took his shot on the table, knocking the eight ball into the side pocket.

•••

Riding through the graveyard always made Rob think about how he was putting his life in grave danger. He understood it was what came with the game, which is why he wanted to get out the game sooner than later. And with the lick he had lined up on Castle, Rob figured it would bring in the money he needs to reach his goal of stacking a million dollars.

Arriving at his stash spot, Rob parked the Hellcat and then grabbed up his bag of money and shovel before stepping out. As he approached the burial grounds, he noticed that not too far away, there was a fresh gravesite marked with a cross tombstone. He was sure it was another soul loss too early. Little did he know that grave belonged to Don. And ironically, Rob was there to add the 40 Gs he had come up off of Don to his already stashed away money in the grave.

After burying the money, Rob was back in his Hellcat and on his way to TJ's place. But first, he decided that he would stop in the hood to cop some weed. Shortly thereafter, he was in TJ's crib seated on the couch in the front room with a Milwaukee Brewers game showing on the flat screen mounted on the wall. Rob took a pull from the blunt of za before passing it to his right to TJ.

"TJ, you sure about bein' done with the stickup game? I mean, it's your decision," Rob said.

TJ puffed the blunt. "Yeah, I'm sure. This is somethin' I been plannin' to do for a while now. We can't poke niggas forever. At some point, that shit gon' catch up to a nigga. And I wanna be long gone before it has a chance to catch up to me. And so should you, Rob."

"And do what? I have been pokin' niggas so long, I'ont know what else to do with myself."

"Now you startin' to sound like that fool-ass nigga, Bone."
TJ snorted and shook his damn head. "You can do what I plan
to do and invest your money into flippin' houses. That way,
your money will be making money for you, then you won't
need to hit licks."

"You got it all figured out, huh?"

"Not exactly. But it's worth a chance. We take chances of
catchin' a body and/or a bullet every time we mask up. At least
with this chance, I won't be puttin' my life on the line," TJ
expounded.

"And what makes you so sure it'll work, TJ?" Rob pressed.

"I ain't sure. And what makes you so sure the major lick
you got lined up will go as planned?" he asked in turn. "All
I'm sayin' is any chance is risky."

"You right." Rob wanted to get out of the game himself
once he reached his money goal, but he didn't exactly know
what he would do with himself. At some point, he would tell
the gang, but not until he felt the time was right. "Apparently,
Bone doesn't like the idea of you bein' done. He says you
shouldn't even be in on the major lick," he stressed.

"Well, it's not up to Bone. Besides, that nigga would rather not have me in on the lick only because he wants more
gains for himself. And that shit doesn't sit well with me." TJ
hit the blunt once again then passed it to Rob.

"I'm sure Bone only said that shit outta bein' heated in the
moment. We both know he's loyal to us. The same goes for
Max. We've all saved each other's lives before, so those are
two niggas we can trust with our lives," Rob said reassuringly.

TJ reflected upon several times when they all saved each
other's lives during licks and beef. "You're right, but Bone
better watch himself comin' at me with his bullshit."

"You know how Bone is, so don't even worry about his
ass. I just wanna be sure we're all on the same page when it

comes to this major lick." Rob knew that the best way to ensure the lick would be pulled off without a hitch was to have everyone stick together. Or everything could fall apart.

•••

Standing on the shore, Kayla peered out at the lake. She normally came to this particular spot to think. After she and TJ had a disagreement earlier in the day, she needed some time to think things over. There was no doubt that Kayla loved TJ, so she wanted him to know that nothing or no one could come between them. But there seemed to be a wedge between them ever since Bone got out of jail. Kayla could tell that TJ and Bone had unresolved beef. She just didn't want them to beef over her. Little did she know, TJ and Bone's beef was about more than just a bitch. It was also about money.

It was growing later in the evening, and Kayla thought it was best she got home soon. She assumed that TJ might start to wonder where she had headed off to. While peering out at the lake, all of a sudden, a pair of hands covered Kayla's eyes from behind. A smile spread across her lips because she figured it was none other than TJ, being that he was one of the only other people who knew about this particular spot. I should've known that he would come here, Kayla mused.

"Guess who," a voice said into Kayla's ear.

Once Kayla recognized who the voice belonged to, she spun on her heels and replied, "Bone?"

"Good guess," Bone smirked.

Back when they were together, Bone would bring Kayla to this very spot just to be alone with her. The two of them being there in this very moment brought back old memories and feelings for each of them, unbeknownst to each other. They actually had a good thing in the past, but when Bone got locked up, the circumstances unexpectedly changed things once TJ came into the equation. It was never Kayla's intent to leave Bone in order to be with TJ. It's just how things went. And of course, she felt bad about it, but she couldn't control what her heart wanted.

"What are you doing here?" Kayla asked curiously. Bone peered out over the lake. "I ain't stalkin' you if that's what you think. I just came here to get a peace of mind. I wasn't expectin' you to even be here, but obviously, you still remember this spot from when I used to bring you here at times."

"How could I ever forget something so beautiful?"

Bone brought his eyes to hers. "That's exactly how I felt about you while I was on lockdown." He noticed Kayla blush as she looked away. "Kayla, I want you to know that I ain't mad at you. I just don't understand what made you choose TJ over me. But as long as you're happy, then that's all that matters."

"Good to know because I am happy with TJ. And I don't expect you to understand my choice, Bone, but it had nothing to do with me comparing you to TJ at all. Just know that it wasn't an easy choice for me," she expressed.

"I still can't believe TJ made a move on you when he was s'posed to be my nigga. Which is why I'll never trust him again," Bone scoffed.

"Listen, I'm sure that you're still mad with TJ, but I don't want you and him beefing over me because I wouldn't want for anything to happen to either of you."

"Kay, my beef with TJ is about more than just you. And the worse has already happened. He betrayed me. But I don't get mad; I get even," he stated, looking Kayla in the eyes.

Kayla eyed him through slits. "Just don't do anything you'll regret."

"Trust me. I won't."

"I should get going." Kayla turned and headed for her Benz, leaving Bone with his thoughts. As she headed away, Bone admired her ass all the way until she stepped inside the car then drove away.

Bone found himself peering out over the lake, reminiscing about his past with Kayla. He knew it was best to leave the past in the past, although it didn't take away the betrayal he felt from TJ getting with Kayla the way he did. Not to mention that TJ didn't seem to want him back hittin' licks with the gang. Bone thought that since TJ planned to leave the game any-fuckin'-way, then TJ shouldn't be in on the major lick Rob had lined up. The only reason Bone was willing to accept it is because it was all part of his grand scheme. And when the time comes, then Bone would make his move.

Martell "Troublesome" Bolden

CHAPTER 6

The hair salon was bustling, and Trina had just finished up doing a client's sew-in. She was looking forward to seeing her next client, Parker, solely so she could gather as much info on her man for Rob. So far, Trina gathered that he was a ballin' ass dope-boy, yet she needed much more. Parker stepped up and took a seat in Trina's chair, not realizing that she was now in the hot seat.

"Hey, girl!" Trina feigned a smile. "I'm guessing you want the usual done."

"Yes, girl. And make sure you tighten up my edges because I'm sure it needs it most." Parker chuckled.

"I got you, boo." Trina began her process. "So, I saw you get dropped off again by that nigga in the Bentley. Seems like he's taking good care of you," she pried while shampooing Parker's hair.

"He is. And good thing the nigga is having money because a bitch ain't cheap," Parker commented.

"Ain't that the truth!" Trina exclaimed. *It's bitches like you who get your man robbed*, she thought. But instead, she said, "Now, tell me all about this mystery man of yours."

Trina's last client of the day was Parker. After finishing up her hair and cleaning up her hair station, it was time for Trina to get off work. Unlike usual, Rob happened to be on time picking her up. He was seated in the driver's side puffing on a blunt of za while listening to Moneybagg Yo's "Time Today" when she entered the passenger seat of the Hellcat.

"Wanna grab somethin' to eat?" Rob inquired as he pulled off down the street.

"I got something you can eat anytime you want," Trina half-joked, referring to her pussy.

Rob puffed the blunt once more before passing it to her. "Maybe later on for a late-night snack," he smirked.

"I'll hold you to that. Right now, I can go for some tacos."

"Taco Bell it is." He steered the whip towards the nearest Taco Bell.

"So, I gathered some more info on the mark's bitch today."

Rob cut his eyes over at her then said, "And?"

"The bitch told me everything. She told me he isn't the one who moves the product. He's the boss. I can believe it because every time he comes by with her, he's riding in a Bentley or something luxurious. Speaking of, she told me the nigga keep gunmen with him wherever he goes, and the cars he rides in are bulletproof."

"Is that so?" Rob now knew that whenever he and the gang gunned for the mark, then they would have to catch him at the right place and at the right time. He pulled to a stop at the red light on 27th & Atkinson Street.

"Yes, it is. He also bulletproofed the G-wagon he bought for the bitch just in case she ran into any trouble while trafficking drugs for him," Trina informed.

"Did she happen to say what's his name and where he lives?"

"His name's Castle, and he lives in a mini-mansion down on Lake Drive."

"You sure about that, Trina?" he pressed as he pulled off with traffic.

"Yes, I'm sure, or I wouldn't be telling you. Damn, a bitch feels like I'm being interrogated or some shit."

"My bad, Trina. It's just I need every detail on this nigga. Anything else the bitch said that I should know?" Rob asked.

"Not unless you care to hear all about how good the nigga be apparently fuckin' her, too." She hit the blunt while studying his reaction.

"The pillow talk is all I need. Good job, baby girl," he praised her.

Rob turned into the lot of Taco Bell, where he pulled up to the drive-thru. While ordering his and Trina's food, Rob kept his hand on the pistol laying across his lap for any beef.

Trina eyed him through slits. "Rob, sometimes I get the feeling that you just be using a bitch," she said while they awaited their order to be filled.

"It ain't even like that, boo. A nigga got love for your ass." Rob kept his left hand, which was decorated with Don's former Rolly around his wrist, on the Glock while his other hand was gripping her thigh. "You down for me, right?"

"Yes, I am."

"Then just keep gettin' details outta the bitch. And whenever I lay this Castle nigga down, then I'ma make sure you're able to splurge on a new Birkin."

At the service window, Rob paid for their order and then received the bag of food and cups of soft drinks. It wasn't until he was finna pull out of the lot when he realized that this was the very restaurant that he and the gang had murked Don.

Rob glanced down at the Rolly around his wrist and thought, *Looks better on me any-fuckin'-way.*

•••

"Mmmmm... It feels sooo good!" Brittany moaned in pleasure.

"You like that, boo?" Rich crooned.

"Yaaaas!"

Brittany dug her pedicure nails into Rich's back as he dug his hard dick deep into her snug pussy. She loved it when he fucked her, and he enjoyed the feel of her wetness. It was early in the morning, and they were having wake-up sex. After getting home so late last night and finding Brit already asleep, Rich didn't bother to wake her. But this morning, she woke him with kisses all over his neck, which led to them fuckin'.

"Damn girl, this pussy so good to a nigga," Rich groaned as he slipped his hardness back and forth inside her wetness. They shared a kiss, and he gently bit on her lower lip. Brittany rolled Rich onto his back then mounted him. She slid down on his dick and began rotating her hips. Rich palmed her ass and bounced her up and down on his dick.

Brittany tossed her head back in pleasure and moaned, "Oooh... I'm cummmin!" Her juices flowed from her pussy, causing her body to tense up. She began riding the dick faster.

"Oh, shit!" Rich busted a nut, and then Brittany rolled beside him in bed, both breathing heavily and covered in perspiration. He leaned over and pecked her lips, then said, "You did that, boo. I love you."

"I know, right." She shifted towards Rich and studied him a moment. "Why do you love me?"

Rich peered over at her. "Because you don't need a man, but you don't walk around actin' like you don't need one. I love that you're independent, but you ain't against lettin' a man treat you good. And any good man needs a woman like you."

"Good to know. And I do love how good you treat me," Brittany smiled. She noticed he seemed in a different frame of mind. "Rich, are you alright?"

Rich sighed. "Yeah, I'm a'ight. Just got a lot on my mind."

"You can talk to me about it."

"It's Don. Ever since he was killed, shit seems to be on my shoulders."

"Now, you have to find the strength to carry the weight of the game."

"I guess you're right," Rich commended. He kissed her forehead. "What would I do without you?"

"You would be lost," Brittany cracked. "Now lemme get some more of that good dick."

Rich yawned. "I'm tired, so I need to catch some Zs."

"So..." She removed the covers from over her and displayed her naked frame. "You don't want all of this?"

"On second thought, I'm well awake!"

Rich and Brittany began kissing, their tongues in sync. He rolled her onto her back, and she guided his stiff dick deep inside her slippery pussy. They enjoyed the feel of each other.

•••

It had been quite a while since Angie was last in the hood. Ever since Don had helped her get cleaned up and moved her out the hood, she stayed clean and stayed away. But after Don's murder, she had been so stressed and needed to escape reality. Angie stepped onto the front porch of the trap spot and reluctantly knocked on its door, and a moment later, it was pulled open by Swindle.

"Haven't seen you in a while, but I knew you'd stop by," Swindle commented.

"Just need a rock in order to get some shit off my mind," Angie told him.

"Last I heard, you were off the pipe." He noticed that she looked much better than when she was strung out.

Angie threw her hands on her hips and remarked, "Let me worry about my damn sobriety, Swindle."

"Say no more." Swindle stepped aside and allowed her inside.

Before Don had placed Angie into rehab, Swindle was her regular supplier. It was one beef he and Don had, given that

Don had told him to no longer support his mother's crack habit. This led to Swindle putting Rob on Don to have him robbed and killed. Swindle knew if Rich happened to find out, then Rich would come for him, so he needed to also have Rich murked.

Angie sat on the couch with a crack pipe to her lips. She couldn't seem to bring herself to smoke the drug. Part of her was disgusted with herself for even considering relapsing. All she could think of was her sons and how she didn't want to disappoint them. But her heart was heavy with grief and pain. She didn't know where to turn or what to do. *You shouldn't be here doing this right now*, her conscience chided.

Swindle produced a lighter and held its flames near the tip of the pipe. "Go ahead," he said enticingly.

"Maybe I shouldn't be here," Angie considered.

"Don't act like you don't remember how good this shit makes you feel."

Angie hesitantly wrapped her lips around the pipe. Her cheeks got hollow as she sucked on the pipe, inhaling the crack smoke. Instantly, the drug took its course on her. She felt better than she did in a long time as her body became lax. It was back to chasing her first high.

"Now, do somethin' to make me feel good." Swindle palmed her head and guided it down towards his dick.

CHAPTER 7

Unh-unh, I know her ass is not out here like that, Shanta said to herself introspectively at the sight of Kat. She shook her damn head as she parked her Altima at the curb in front of Kat's place, where Parker set on the porch steps.

Kat was talking with her latest catch while she leaned into the driver's window of his candy red Chevy Impala on chrome 26'' rims. She had on a crop top with #BadBitch across the chest, some booty-shorts that crept into the crevice of phat ass, and a pair of Air Jordan's. Kat had no shame in her game.

"Hey, Shan," Parker greeted once Shanta stepped out of the car.

"Hey, girl. I see Kat done caught herself another dawg-ass nigga," Shanta quipped as she made her way towards the porch. Kat turned to them and said, "Shan, c'mere. There's someone who wants to meet you. And he's fine."

"No, thanks," Shanta declined, not wanting shit to do with whoever the nigga is in the passenger seat of the Impala.

"Shorty, why don't you come here for a minute," the passenger called out.

"Boy, I don't want no bum who can't do nothing for me. So, stop hanging out the passenger side of your homeboy whip trying to shoot your shot at me," she clowned his ass.

"Whatever," the passenger sat back in his seat, humbled.

Shanta turned her attention to Parker. "Anyway, girl," she sighed.

"How're things for you, Shan?" asked Parker.

"Things are getting better. I mean, I'm dealing with the loss of Don and our baby better than before. I guess I'm just trying to move on without feeling guilty."

"Girl, just because you move on it doesn't mean you have to forget about Don and the baby. However, it's best that you move on for the sake of yourself."

"Trust me. I'm trying," Shanta uttered. Parker could tell that it was hard for her to move on with her life. She just hoped that Shan eventually learned how.

Kat came making her way towards her girls as the Impala pulled off down the street. "Shan, your ass didn't have to clown ol' boy like that. He seemed like a good nigga," she said with a hint of attitude.

"Bitch, please. The nigga wasn't even worth my time," Shanta replied.

"Nigga probably several bitches baby's daddy and don't nobody need that baby mama drama in their life like you," Parker added.

Kat waved her off and said, "Ever since you got yourself a new man, you've been acting brand-new with niggas anyway. And Shan, you need to get yourself a new man."

"Kat, you don't even have yourself a man. Instead, you fuck everyone else's. Besides, I'm just taking things slow for now when it comes to finding a man," Shanta replied.

"Well, I ain't into taking it slow."

"Bitch, anyway. What do y'all wanna get into today?" Shan asked.

"How about we hit the mall up?" Parker suggested.

"I like the sound of that," Kat seconded.

Shanta stood and said, "Let's bounce." She headed for the whip with her girls in tow.

After leaving the mall with numerous shopping bags from different outlets, the girls were back in traffic with Latto's "On God" blaring from the speakers.

Kat did a little twerk in her seat to the music. "See, me and Latto are just alike. We both treat niggas like they ain't shit," she commented.

"Only thing you have in common with her is a big ass," Shan jeered, causing Parker to laugh. She pulled to a stoplight.

"And I use my assets to get what I want outta niggas."

"Kat, when are you going to learn that most niggas don't trust a big ass and a smile," Shan said.

"Trust me, all niggas like a bitch with a big ass."

"I know mine do!" Parker added and high-fived Kat.

"And since you need a nigga of your own, me and Parker gonna help you find one. So, we're going out this weekend," Kat told Shanta.

"Unh-unh, Katherine, I ain't going out," Shan objected. "On top of that, I don't even have anything to wear."

"Bitch, you going. And I ain't taking no for an answer. You can wear that cute little Fendi outfit you just picked up at the mall."

"It'll be fun, Shan," Parker inputted. Besides, we haven't been out since..." Her words trailed off.

"Since Don was killed and all," Shanta completed Parker's words. "Maybe I do need to go out." She never imagined herself being without Don, and now she was considering moving on.

"Then no more excuses. This weekend we're going out!" Kat encouraged. She turned up the volume to the music, and the girls all began to have a little dance party in their seats.

The girls stopped at a cute little café located downtown. As Shanta, Kat, and Parker entered the establishment, they had come upon Brittany. It had been a while since Shan and Brit saw one another during the funeral.

"Hey there, girl!" Shanta greeted with excitement.

"Hey!" Brittany and Shanta shared a hug. "Long time no see."

"I know, right. Lemme introduce you to my girls here. This is Kat, and that's Parker," she pointed at each of her girls. "And girls, this is Brittany, Rich's girlfriend."

"Nice to meet both of you."

Parker waved and said, "Likewise."

"S'cuse me," Kat scoffed as she walked away and flipped her long weave over her shoulder. She wasn't impressed with Rich's girlfriend and thought he could do better.

"Don't mind her. She just has to warm up to people," Shanta assured.

"Shan's right about that," Parker added. "Well, I'll leave you two alone. Nice meeting you, girl." She went on her way to catch up with Kat.

"Thanks for introducing me to your girls."

"They're cool once you get to know them."

"I'm sure. So, how have you been since I have last seen you?"

Shan sighed. "Still trying to cope with the loss and all."

"Girl," Brit rubbed Shanta's arm in solace, "you just have to live your best life."

"The best life I could've ever had would've been with Don and our baby. Now I don't know what am I to do with my life."

"Just remember that life is what you make it."

"True. And how's life been for Rich?" Shanta inquired.

"He's been living each day the best he can. I can see that it hasn't been easy for him either, and all I can do is comfort him," Brittany told her.

"Even though he and Don had their differences, Rich loved his brother regardless. So, losing Don will affect Rich's life forever. I just hope that it doesn't affect your relationship with him."

"Well, I do know how he loved Don no matter what. I care about Rich a lot, so I'll be there for him as much as he needs me, and through that, I hope it strengthens our relationship moving forward."

"I'm sure it will. And I'm sure it will bring you closer to Angie because she really loves her sons."

"I can tell that she does. Speaking of, have you seen Angie lately?"

"No. For some reason, I just can't seem to bring myself to see her. I guess it's because I survived, yet Don and the baby didn't. So, part of me feels guilty," Shanta expressed.

Brittany could see tears in her eyes. "Well, there's no reason for you to feel guilty. I believe it's best that you go and see Angie. I'm sure she'd love that."

"You're right. I'll make time to go and see her soon."

"And if you'd like, I'll come with you," Brit offered.

"No, thank you. Maybe it's best that I go alone," Shanta replied. "But how about you stay and chat with us girls?"

"Sorry, I would like to, but I have to get back to work. Maybe some other time."

"Then I'll catch you later." Shanta offered her a hug before they went their separate ways. She found her way to the table that her girls occupied and took a seat in the vacant chair.

Parker said, "Rich's girl seems nice."

"She is," Shanta agreed.

"Rich can do better than that bitch," Kat scoffed.

"Lemme guess, you would be better for him than her," Shanta replied sarcastically. "Kat, get over yourself. Rich is happy with Brittany, and I think she's good for him. Anyways, let's order."

•••

"Hell is she doin' here?"

Heavy had come to the trap spot to check on shit, and when he stepped inside, he noticed Angie there with Swindle. He didn't like the sight of Angie being in the spot ass naked with a pipe in her mouth, smoking crack. In fact, after falling off the wagon, she'd been there for nearly a week on a crack binge. Heavy noticed she looked high outta her mind, and he figured after Don was murdered, she just wanted to ease her pain. But Swindle used her for his personal gain.

"Swindle, if Rich finds out she's here, then there's bound to be a problem. Especially after Don helped her get sober, and now you're enablin' her relapse," Heavy said disapprovingly.

Swindle was seated on the couch counting cash, which was spread out on the coffee table. "Last I checked, she's a grown-ass woman and can do what she wants. Besides, Don ain't here to feel a way about it, and Rich doesn't scare me!" he retorted.

"Dawg, don't you see how Rich is willin' to go hard for Don, and you don't think he'll do the same for their mama? I ain't finna be part of what's goin' on here with Angie."

"Nigga!" Swindle jumped to his feet. "You actin' like Rich got you hoin' up or some shit. Ain't our damn fault that his mama smokes crack; we're just the supplier. Regardless, she'll get it from someone else if not us."

"Then let her ass get it from someone else. After you finish countin' up the money, I want her ass outta here, Swindle," Heavy told him. "And let's get one thing straight. It ain't no hoe in my flesh." He turned for the door.

Swindle stared daggers at Heavy's back as Heavy made his way out the door. Resentfully Swindle thought, *We'll see about that, hoe-ass nigga.*

•••

Max pulled his Audi to a stop at the red light on Humboldt and Burleigh Street. "So, I left the lil bitch on read, and she started trollin' me on the 'Gram and shit," he was saying. "Then I—"

"Nigga, do I look like I give a fuck about your social media drama?" Bone hissed, cutting Max short of his story. "Enough about that shit. What you think about the nigga, TJ, talkin' 'bout bein' done with hittin' licks all of a sudden? I ain't feelin' that shit."

"Ain't shit that can be done about it. So, if TJ wants to be done, then that's on him," Max replied.

Bone shifted towards him. "What if there is somethin' that can be done about it?"

"Like what?" Max asked with a quirked brow.

"We tell Rob either he cuts TJ outta the major move he has lined up, or we won't participate. Don't you get it? Without TJ, then we stand to see more paper from this move. Besides, we don't need his ass there if all he's gonna do is take the money and run," he explained.

"Bone, we both know that Rob ain't finna just cut TJ out. And as much as I'ont like the fact that TJ's talkin' 'bout bein' done, I gotta hit that lick 'cause I need the money. Even still, you know I'm down for you."

"Then how 'bout we hit the lick ourselves without Rob and TJ? We don't need them. That way, you and I can split the money," Bone suggested.

"But they're our boys, and I ain't willin' to cut them out over money," Max objected.

Bone sat back in his seat. "You know what, just forget I ever even mentioned it."

The light flipped green, and Max pulled off with traffic. He and Bone were on their way to meet with Rob and TJ. What Max failed to realize is Bone had been plotting on branching off from the gang for a while now. Bone figured that by pulling capers with fewer niggas it would mean a bigger pay. Bone had hoped Max would be on board because he'd rather not have to cut him out also. Bone had been loyal to the gang since day one, but greed had its way of evolving into treachery.

CHAPTER 8

In the VIP section, Rich and T-Mac were seated on the huge purple suede wraparound couch alongside Heavy and Swindle, who also had some of their crew lounging around. They were enjoying the scene and bottle service. Rich thought it was best to meet with Heavy once again in order to set things straight before they did any business.

Rich shifted towards Heavy. "Look, if we're gonna deal with each other, then I'ont want any funny business," he insisted.

Heavy turned up the bottle of Ace of Spade to his lips. "Rich, ain't shit funny about this business we're in. If a nigga don't take it seriously, then he's bound to get himself indicted or murdered. And I ain't lookin' forward to neither," he assured.

"Agreed. Now that we have that understood, I have all the papers together for the work. Just name the time and place."

"Look, how 'bout we focus on gettin' lit for the rest of the night, and I'll get at you tomorrow with the details."

"Actually, I ain't big into the club scenes, so I'll leave you to it." Rich polished off his drink before heading towards the exit with T-Mac in tow.

"It's somethin' about that nigga I like," Heavy told Swindle. "But I know he could turn out to be a threat."

"Just gimme the word, and he's a goner," Swindle declared. Besides, he knew that if Rich was to find out who murked Don, then it would ruin his plot, so Swindle had to put his plot in motion ASAP.

"That's not necessary, as long as he don't get bigger than me."

Swindle just shook his damn head at how unaware Heavy was and then sipped at his bottle of Rosé.

As Rich and T-Mac stepped towards the exit, Rich noticed Shanta entering the club with her homegirls, Parker and Kat. Shan was looking like a snack in her red body-hugging track-suit and sneakers that were all designed by Fendi. Her hair was in soft baby doll curls, her makeup was light, and the only accessories she wore were gold hooped earrings with her Rolex.

"Apparently, you feelin' much better seein' that you're out tonight," Rich suggested.

"Not exactly. I only came because my girls practically dragged my ass out the house," Shan replied. "How about you, are you okay?"

"Tryin' to be, but it's not so easy."

Shanta sighed. "I know, right. Just know that I'm always here for you."

"I know. Well, at least you should enjoy the night," he told her.

"Leaving already? Thought maybe you and your boy would like to have some drinks with me and my girls."

"I'd like that, but I'll have to some other time. Enjoy yourself." Rich made his way out, followed by T-Mac.

•••

Rob, TJ, Max, and Bone occupied a table in VIP, enjoying the atmosphere as music blared from the club's subwoofers while bitches twerked, bottles were popped, and weed smoke was put in the air. Rob thought it was a good idea for the gang to kick it with the hopes of putting their differences behind them.

Rob leaned back in his seat. "You know, we been through a lot of shit together, and I want y'all to know that it shouldn't be shit that can come between us," he said to the gang.

"Facts," Max concurred.

Rob went on, "We all we got, and without each other, we ain't gang. Our guns are only for our opps. Feel me?" He peered at TJ and then Bone.

"Yeah, we good," TJ responded.

"Fa sho." Bone dapped up Rob.

"That's whassup!" Max exclaimed.

A bottle girl, who was a thick-ass redbone with long red hair and numerous tatts, brought over four bottles of bubbly to their table in a bucket of ice. "These are on your friend there," she referred to Heavy. After delivering the bottles and receiving a hefty tip, the bottle girl strutted away with the whole gang admiring her phat ass.

Rob grabbed one of the bottles and raised it. "To the gang."

The others also raised a bottle in toast. They each clinked bottles and took a drink of the bubbly. Rob stood and said, "Yo, I'm finna go and holla at Heavy's fat-ass real quick." He made his way over to Heavy's table.

"And where you headed?" Max asked as Bone rose to his feet.

"Gotta take a piss," Bone remarked before turning for the restroom.

TJ shook his damn head. "Somethin' seems off with Bone's ass."

"Yeah, I know what you mean," Max replied and then took a drink from his bottle.

"Is there somethin' you ain't tellin' us about Bone that you know?" TJ probed, eyeing him through slits.

"N-naw, man. It's just Bone hasn't seemed himself since he got outta jail," Max deceived. He considered against mentioning that Bone had brought up the idea of cutting out Rob and TJ in order to avoid there being bad blood amongst the gang. But then again, maybe it was best that he did mention it, he considered.

"Yeah, I know, and Rob can't seem to see that." TJ figured there was more, but he decided to let it be.

Max shifted towards him. "Rob just wants all of us to stick together. I'm sure shit won't ever exactly be the same with you and Bone, but that doesn't mean you two have to have bad blood."

"Look, I ain't the one holdin' a damn grudge. If Bone has a problem with me, then he can either solve it or let it be."

"Aside from the other shit, Bone's problem with you is your plan to leave the game. I understand where he's comin' from."

TJ leaned back in his seat. "Thought you'd understand my decision to get out the game before it's too late. Actually, I was hopin' it encourages all of you to do the same. But apparently, y'all plan to be in the game until it claims you. Well, no matter how any of you feel about it, once we hit the major lick Rob has lined up, I'm done," he declared defiantly.

"Then it is what it is." Max began to think that maybe Bone was right about cutting out TJ.

Meanwhile, Rob made his way over to rap with Heavy. With the bottle of bubbly in hand, he approached the huge wraparound couch and took a seat beside the drug boss. He offered Swindle a mean mug, who returned it before rising to his feet and then stepping away, leaving the two alone.

"Wasn't expectin' to see you here tonight," Rob said.

"Had to meet with someone. Plus, I thought I'd come snatch up a couple of these freak hoes," Heavy replied. He took a drink from his bottle of Ace. "So, when can I expect you to drop by with more work?"

"Actually, I have a major lick on deck as we speak. A nigga that I've been lurkin' on for a lil while, and I'm sure layin' his ass down will be big for us both."

"Big like how?" Heavy was eager to know.

"At least ten keys." Rob turned up the bottle to his lips.

"What makes you so sure about this lick?" Skepticism could be detected in Heavy's tone.

Rob eyed him and said, "You let me focus on the lick. Just have your cash right." He sat the bottle of bubbly on the lounge table. "'Preciate the bottles, but personally, I'd prefer Hen."

"Then next time I know," Heavy replied.

"Next time, bottles on me." Rob stood and then headed off.

•••

Shanta, Parker, and Kat were seated at the bar. Of them all, Shan couldn't seem to enjoy herself. She didn't much care to be there. Kat and Parker thought it was best to finally get Shan's ass to come out in the hopes of finding her a new man. However, Shan was doubtful there would be any nigga present who would interest her. So, she was just looking forward to enjoying the night on the town with her bitches.

"Still can't believe that I let you two talk me into coming out tonight," Shan commented.

Kat sipped at her glass of Remy. "You're here now, so you might as well try to get with one of these ballin'-ass niggas walking through," she suggested. "Speaking of, I see a baller over in VIP that needs my attention." She drowned her drink before heading towards the VIP section.

Parker just shook her head. "That girl is something else," she chuckled.

"Ain't that the truth," Shan concurred.

A crew of niggas came walking through and checking the girls out. Shanta displayed apparent disinterest, and Parker noticed her vibe.

"See any nigga you're interested in?" Parker asked.

"All I see is a lot of thirsty niggas."

"Girl, you are a tough sale."

"Only because I'm worth a lot," Shan replied. "I need myself a drink." She waved over the barkeeper and ordered herself a dirty martini.

"It's on me," a smooth voice said that belonged to Rob. He took up the vacant stool beside the gorgeous Shanta. "And, barkeeper, while you at it, pour me up a double shot of Hennessey."

Shanta laid eyes on the tall, brown skin nigga with brown eyes and a crisp bald fade. He was dressed to impress, rockin' a button-up, jeans, and sneakers all designed by Balenciaga. Not to mention, she noticed he sported a very familiar Rolex. *Damn girl, he's fine,* her conscience mused. She said, "I appreciate the gesture, but I'll pass."

"Then I'll take it as an insult." Rob smiled.

Shan studied him a moment. "And what are you expecting in return?"

Rob shook his head. "Just 'cause a nigga buy a bad bitch a drink doesn't mean he expects anything in return. But a thank you would be cool."

"Then, no, thank you for the drink," she replied. Parker gave her a subtle nudge before stepping away.

The barkeeper set their drinks on the bar before them. Rob grabbed up his and took a swig. "The drinks are already paid for, so you're welcome," he rebutted, wearing a smile. "My name's Rob. And yours?"

Bitch, he was nice enough to buy you a drink. The least you could do is give him your damn name, her conscience suggested. "Shanta. But my friends call me Shan."

"Nice to meet you, Shanta. Now, I'll let you enjoy your drink alone." Rob began to rise from his bar stool when Shanta decided to stop him.

"How about you stay and I enjoy my drink in your company," Shanta proposed with a smile. "And you can call me Shan." She then took a sip of her martini. Neither weren't aware of who the other was. If only they knew.

•••

After using the restroom, Bone was on his way out when he happened to come across Swindle. The two weren't exactly friends, although they were associates.

"Just the nigga I wanna holla at," Swindle said with a smirk.

"Fuck, you wanna holla at me about?" Bone pressed.

"Not now, not around them," he referred to the Heavy and Rob. "But if you're interested in makin' some more paper, then you'll meet up with me at Final Detailing tomorrow at noon," Swindle told him before going on his way, leaving Bone to make a decision.

As Bone headed back towards the table, he noticed Rob over at the bar entertaining some bitch. *Nigga just don't know what's comin',* he thought, seething.

Martell "Troublesome" Bolden

CHAPTER 9

The barista served Shanta and her girls their drinks. They then found themselves a small table in the café. Though it was nearly noon, they could use some caffeine after hanging out so damn late last night.

Shanta sipped at her mocha latte. "Kat, I noticed you slipped out the club on us last night with some baller. Girl, you don't waste no time giving it up," she half-joked.

"FYI, I'm a grown-ass bitch, so I can give this pussy up to whoever I want, whenever I want," Kat sassed and flipped her long sew-in weave back over her shoulder.

"Excuse me, do you, boo-boo," Shanta chuckled.

"So Shan, what happened with ol' boy that you were vibing with last night? Is he your type?" Parker inquired and then took a sip of her cappuccino.

"Yeah, don't act like we didn't see you all up in that nigga's face, smiling all hard and shit. Apparently, you were feeling what's-his-name. Maybe you should've left with him," Kat added.

Shanta leaned back in her seat and crossed her legs. "His name's Rob. And if I'm being honest, I liked him a lot. I enjoyed his vibe, and he actually impressed me with how he was street yet modest. I'm interested in getting to know more of who he is." If only she knew that he was one who had taken Don.

Parker gasped. "Shan, girl, are you blushing right now just thinking about Rob? Bitch, you are." She noticed Shanta's cheeks were rosy red.

"Sure, you didn't give it up," Kat commented.

"Kat, now you know I don't get down like that. It's just Rob seems like a good nigga. One that I can possibly move on with from Don," Shanta replied.

"Did you tell him about Don at all?" Parker inquired.

Shan shook her head. "No. But if things grow serious between us, then I will. As of now, I just want to know him better."

"Well, good. Because now maybe we can all go out on a group date with our niggas," Kat chimed in.

"Speaking of, when do we finally get to meet this Castle, Parker?" Shan wanted to know.

"Right. Because you been keeping his ass away from us." Kat placed a hand on Parker's arm and half-joked, "Girl, it's okay if he's ugly, as long as he has some coins. We ain't judging."

Shanta laughed while shaking her head at Kat.

"Whatevs, Kat. Castle is not ugly at all. I just hope that y'all will like him," Parker said.

"Parker, since you like him as much as you do, then I'm sure we will also," Shanta told her.

"Hope so. As a matter of fact, I'm supposed to be meeting up with him for lunch. I'll get with you two later. Smooches." Parker grabbed up her Birkin bag and drink, then headed for the door.

Kat took a sip of her iced coffee. "Have you peeped that her ass been jumping lately ever since meeting this Castle nigga. Or is it just me?"

"No, I've peeped it too. Maybe she just wants to show him that she's there for him," Shan responded.

"Maybe."

•••

Rob and Trina were sitting on the loveseat in the front room of her apartment. They were smoking on a blunt of za while she informed him of the latest information that she had solicited from Parker about his mark, Castle.

"And she told you this shit herself?" Rob pressed eagerly. He took a pull on the blunt.

"Yep. She said Castle plans to have her pick up the largest load she's trafficked for him so far," Trina informed.

"Did she say how large?"

"No. Only that she picks it up and then takes it straight to Castle."

"Say no more." Rob had an idea how to use Parker to his advantage in laying down Castle.

Trina shifted towards him. "Enough about that. I want to ask you something."

"Ask." He puffed the blunt.

"How do you really feel about us, Rob?"

Rob shook his damn head and replied, "Trina, you know a nigga got love for your ass."

"Don't come at me with that love shit when you don't even take us serious, okay?" She displayed an attitude.

"What is this about?" Rob figured there had to be more to her attitude problem.

Trina eyed him through slits and said, "Nigga, I heard about you at the club all up in some bitch's face and shit."

"Are you fa real with this shit right now, Trina?" Rob breathed.

"Fa real, fa real. So, who was the bitch, Rob?" she pressed.

This bitch needs to know her place, Rob thought. "Check it out, you ain't my bitch, and whatever bitch I fuck with isn't your concern, Trina. So just play your role and leave the feelings out of it. A'ight?" He puffed the blunt and then dumped its ashes in the tray on the coffee table.

Trina folded her arms with an attitude and pouted. "Alright, whatever, Rob." She held feelings for him, even though she knew they weren't together. But what is a bitch supposed to feel when Rob always laid up with her, fuckin' her good and shit? Trina just wanted him to love her.

"Trina, listen," Rob began gingerly. He could read that her feelings were hurt. "You've been holdin' me down for a while. So, of course, a nigga got love for you. Now, girl, gimme that pussy."

Rob pulled her close and kissed her. As heated as Trina was with him, she just couldn't resist him. He slid a hand inside her Chanel leggings, then slipped fingers inside her wetness, and caused her to moan. She kissed him hungrily and gently bit on his lower lip as he helped her out of her leggings. Pulling her fitted T-shirt off over her head and exposing her titties, Rob sucked and licked on her erect nipples. His warm mouth on her felt so damn wonderful. Trina undid his Amiri jeans then pulled out his hard dick. She straddled his lap, sliding her wet-shot down on his erection.

"Damn Trina, this shit so wet!" Rob grunted as she rode him. He palmed her ass and lifted her up to the tip of his dick, and slammed her back down to its base repetitively while he sucked and licked her hard nipples.

Trina tossed back her head in pleasure. "Ooh, Rob, you hitting... my spot!" She felt her pussy cum all over his dick. "Yeesss... That's it right there!"

Rob rose from the loveseat holding Trina up by her phat ass, and Trina wrapped her legs around him. He began to drill his dick back and forth in her pussy. Rob enjoyed the feel of Trina's slippery walls gripping at his stiff tool. As Rob dug himself deep in her, Trina dug her designer manicure into his back. He lay her back on the loveseat and positioned her legs on his shoulders as he fucked her, and she enjoyed how his dick filled her.

"Aww, shit... A nigga about ready to bust!" Rob groaned. Feeling himself on the verge of bustin' a nut, he pulled his dick out from her pussy and shot semen on her belly. Afterwards, he took a seat beside her, both panting from good fuckin'. "Shit, boo, a nigga definitely got love for you," he said, catching his breath.

"Nigga, whatevs. All you got love for is this pussy," Trina half-joked.

Rob eyed her. "Pussy will never be my downfall."

•••

Fuck this nigga want with me on some low-key shit, Bone mused in regards to Swindle as he turned the Yukon onto the grounds of the auto detailing shop. Admittedly, he was interested in finding out what Swindle meant the last night at the club about him being able to make more money. Bone understood that more money meant more problems, but it was nothing his gun couldn't solve.

Swindle was talking into his iPhone while leaning back up against his Chrysler, which was being detailed by customer services. He peeped Bone's whip pull up then ended his call. *If this nigga knows what's good for him, then he'll fall in line*, Swindle contemplated. Before Bone could step outta his ride, Swindle pulled open its passenger door and then stepped inside. Immediately, Swindle noticed the pole fitted with a thirty-shot stick laying across Bone's lap.

"Dawg, fuck do you wanna rap with me about?" Bone inquired curiously, keeping a hand rested on his pole.

"About money," Swindle answered.

Bone eased up. "I'm listenin'."

"Look, you can either continue to let that nigga Rob do business with Heavy, or you can do business with me. The way I see it, both them niggas gettin' more money outta the deals than we are. So how 'bout we cut 'em out, and from now on, you bring me the product, and I'll pay you the money. The only thing is, we'll have to be willin' to make sure our business stays between us. Na' mean?" Swindle gave him a telling look.

"Yeah, I know what you mean," Bone replied, with full understanding.

"Cool. Be in touch." Swindle stepped outta the Yukon, leaving Bone with his thoughts.

Bone had to admit that Swindle's business proposal was how he would prefer things. Although he knew that if he was to cut out Rob, then it was either kill or be killed. And as for the money on their heads, before he decided to off Rich, he figured that he might be able to use it to his advantage in one way or another.

CHAPTER 10

Led by a nigga with a pistol protruding from his waist, Rich, along with T-Mac, entered the trap spot, where they were to meet with Heavy. Inside the basement, Heavy stood near the pool table with Swindle. Rich approached and then tossed the Burberry backpack atop the table, interrupting the game of pool.

"There's the money, now where's the bricks," Rich requested.

Heavy grabbed the backpack, unzipped it, and then dumped the numerous stacks of rubber band bankrolls out on the tabletop and said, "Cash on delivery." He nodded at Swindle, who then stepped away for a moment before returning with the three kilos and sat them on the table. "Nice doin' business with you."

"Dawg, not so fast. You checked the paper. Now we'll check the work," T-Mac piped in.

"Go right ahead," Swindle told them.

Rich materialized a pocketknife and then cut into the packaged brick of coke, and he could tell the dope was high-quality fish scale. Its Libra logo stamped on the kilo immediately caught Rich's eye, for it was the stamp on the bricks Don copped from his plug. Without words, Rich pulled his Glock from his waist and then aimed at Heavy. Following suit, T-Mac drew his Tec-9 and brandished it about the room, daring any of the others to move. As one of Heavy's goons reached for his own pole, then T-Mac let off.

Prraat, prraat!

After the goon was riddled with bullets, then the others didn't dare make a move. Heavy didn't understand what the hell was going on. He didn't know what had gotten into Rich.

"What the hell, Rich?!" Heavy cried out, holding his hands up.

"Nigga, this whole fuckin' time, your ass had somethin' to do with my brother being murked!" Rich raged, ready to pop a slug in Heavy's dome.

Heavy looked confused. "Fuck are you talkin' 'bout?"

"I'm talkin' 'bout these bricks. They belonged to Don."

"What? How do you figure that shit?"

Rich grabbed up one of the bricks and threw it at Heavy's chest. "I can tell by the fuckin' stamp on the bricks," he explained.

"Rich, on my word, I didn't know," Heavy replied pleadingly.

"Where'd you get the bricks?" After a moment of silence, Rich became overcome with rage. "I want a fuckin' answer, now!"

"Rich, if I tell you, then the nigga will murk me."

Rich pressed the muzzle to his dome and stated, "And if you don't, then I will."

Swindle piped in, "The nigga who sold us the bricks is Rob."

Rich turned his aim on Swindle. "Who'd you say the nigga is?"

"Rob is the nigga you should be lookin' for." Swindle understood that he could use Rich to get Rob out the way.

"Maybe y'all had somethin' to do with settin' up Don to be murked," he accused.

"Then why the fuck would I try to sell you the work if I knew it belonged to Don?" Heavy reasoned. He knew that if Rich believed he had anything to do with Don's murder, then he was dead on the spot. "Rich, I didn't set up your brother."

"Then tell me where I can find the nigga Rob," Rich demanded, returning the muzzle to Heavy's dome.

"I'ont know. The nigga just drops by whenever he has work for sale. Listen, Rob isn't part of my gang, so he isn't my concern."

Rich allowed his gun to fall at his side. "A'ight. But if I find out you did have somethin' to do with Don bein' murked, I'ma be sure to put a slug in your noggin." He began tossing the cash and birds inside the backpack. "And since you're in my debt, I'm takin' all of this shit without complaint."

"So, you just gonna rob me like that?"

"A fair exchange ain't a robbery." As Rich made his way out, T-Mac followed while backpedaling and holding his Tec-9 leveled. Now that he knew who the nigga was that had a hand in murkin' Don, Rich would set out to spill Rob's blood.

Back at their main trap spot in the hood that Rich and his gang operated, they were in the kitchen seated around the table. Rich removed each kilo from the backpack and tossed them atop the table. Immediately, C-note and Danger knew the bricks had belonged to Don by the Libra stampings. T-Mac paced the floor; he was ready to get revenge.

"Got these bricks from Heavy. Claims a nigga named Rob sold 'em to him, so whoever Rob is had somethin' to do with Don bein' murked," Rich said.

"I'ont think it was a good idea to let the nigga Heavy live. More than likely, he'll let Rob know you're after his ass," T-Mac voiced.

"For now, we'll just use Heavy for supply. And if he does let Rob know, then let's hope he come after me and make shit easy on us to find his ass. Meantime, we gotta get the traps back jumpin'."

"So, we take these birds and flip 'em. And since I already have shit established, I'll see to it that the work is moved," C-note piped in.

"And whoever the nigga Rob is, he has another fuckin' thing comin' if he thinks he's gonna get away with robbin' and killin' Don," Danger declared.

"We don't even know who his ass is, so how are we gonna go about findin' him?" T-Mac wanted to know.

Rich leaned back in his seat. "Put the word out that I got a brick on his ass and have every killa in the city tryna look for his ass."

•••

Rob pulled up in the hood and parked his Hellcat at the curb in front of the weed spot. It was night out, and with most of the light poles shot out, the block was mostly shrouded with darkness. He tucked his pole in the waist of his Blue Bands Only denim jeans before stepping out the whip and heading for the spot. Subsequent to coppin' himself an ounce of exotic, Rob exited the spot into the gangway and crossed paths with a nigga from around the way named Tray. He wasn't exactly cool with Tray, but they had no beef.

"Yo Rob, lemme holla at you real quick," said Tray.

"Hell you wanna holla at me about?" Rob responded, sounding annoyed.

"I'ont know if you heard, but word is a nigga put a brick on your head, and it has to do with you and your gang havin' somethin' to do with the nigga Don bein' murked."

"That right?" This was the first Rob heard of the bounty, and he wasn't surprised that he was hearing it from Tray of all people. However, he didn't know how true it was. "So, what, you intend to collect that reward?" Rob wanted to know.

"Depends."

Tray whipped out his .9mm and leveled it on Rob's top, and stated, "You can either pay me off or pay in blood."

"Lemme give you some advice. When you pull a pole on someone, make sure you take the fuckin' safety off," Rob told him. He drew his own pole and aimed at Tray's chest.

Blam, blam!

After blammin' Tray twice in the chest, Rob left his ass in the gangway fighting for his worthless life. He didn't need Tray coming after him along with others. As Rob sped away in the Hellcat, his thoughts went 100mph. He had to figure out who the fuck had put a brick on his head for Don and then murk him too.

•••

The gang of jack-boys were gathered in the parking lot of the Diamond Inn. Rob had called the others there, and he knew it was best that they be made aware of the bounty on out on him. Plus, they needed to figure who was on to them and how.

"Fuck you mean Tray told you there's a bounty out on your head?" TJ asked, upset.

"And only one brick?" Max scoffed. "Figured comin' for any of our heads would be worth more than that."

Rob puffed the blunt of za. "Tray told me it had to do with that nigga Don we murked. Thing is shouldn't no one else know 'bout it besides us," he replied suggestively.

"Rob, are you askin' if one of us been runnin' our mouths about the lick?" Bone pointed out.

"How would anyone else know it was us?"

"How about Heavy? Maybe he said somethin' to someone," Max added.

"Yeah, maybe. But he doesn't have reason to say much since we're helpin' him get paid," Rob figured.

"Then maybe he at least knows who put the bounty out," TJ suggested.

Rob turned for the Hellcat and said, "So let's go and see if he knows anything."

They pulled up to Heavy's trap spot and, all strapped with poles, and hopped out their vehicles. Heavy figured that Rob would show up with a purpose at some point. He was seated at the mini-bar alongside Swindle when Rob and the gang entered.

"I take it that you didn't come here to do business," Heavy said to Rob. He took a swig from his glass of Henny.

"Heavy, outside of my boys, you're the only mu'fucka who could even tie me into that nigga Don gettin' murked. My guess is you know exactly who put out the price tag on my head," Rob replied heatedly.

"Look, all I know is the nigga came to cop some work, and just so happen the bricks you last sold me belonged to Don, who's his brother."

"Who's the nigga?" Rob pressed.

"It's not my place to tell." Heavy wasn't willing to take sides in Rob and Rich's beef.

Rob drew his pole and held it dangling at his side. "On everything I stand for, if you don't tell me who the fuck the nigga is, then I'ma put you in a place you don't wanna be, a'ight!" he growled.

"A'ight, take it easy," Swindle chimed in. "The nigga name's Rich. Said he knew those were Don's bricks by the stamp on them." He knew it was in his best interest to have Rob go after Rich.

Rob looked to Heavy and told him, "Only reason I ain't gonna smoke your ass is because you didn't know shit would turn out this way."

"Your beef is between you and Rich. Our business is between you and me," Heavy replied.

Rob replaced the Glock on his waist. "Then, from now on, keep our business between us if you don't want beef." He turned for the door, and the gang followed.

Outside, the gang stood near their vehicles. They needed to figure out how to go about shit moving forward.

"We gotta take out whoever the nigga Rich is before shit gets hectic in the streets with niggas gunnin' for us," Rob told the gang.

"Let niggas come, and I'ma put in gun work," Bone piped in.

"Straight up," Max agreed.

TJ said, "I think it's best that we lay low until we figure this shit out."

Rob looked at him. "TJ, we gonna figure out what's goin' on, but we ain't gonna let this shit prevent us from hittin' the lick." He leaned back up against the whip. "Speakin' of, I got more details on our mark. Now, all we gotta do is lurk on the nigga and watch his every move before we move on his ass."

"And what we gonna do about this shit with Rich in the meantime?" TJ wanted to know.

Rob patted the Glock on his waist. "We'll just have to stay strapped in these streets. And when we find Rich, then we'll murk 'em, just like we did Don."

Martell "Troublesome" Bolden

CHAPTER 11

Answering the knock at the front door, Shanta found Rich standing there holding a bag of Chinese take-out. He had texted her earlier that he would be dropping by. She knew he was just trying to check in on her, which she didn't mind. They cared to remain close, mainly on the strength of Don.

Shanta allowed Rich inside and then locked the door behind him. They stepped into the front room. Shanta sat on the loveseat with her legs folded beneath her while Rich took a seat on the couch then set out the food on the coffee table.

"How you?" Rich asked.

Shanta grabbed up some of the shrimp-fried rice with her chopsticks. "Not so bad. And you?"

"Tryna make it."

"By the way, how's Angie?"

Rich hunched forward and let out a sigh. "I really can't say. She seems to be takin' the loss of Don well, although I'm sure it's heavy on her heart. Don was like her backbone, and without him..."

"Now you'll have to be," Shanta added. She looked at him carefully. "Angie's gonna need you more than you know."

"And I'll be there for her," Rich assured. Little did he know, Angie was in need of him now more than ever.

"I sure do hope so," she said sincerely.

"Listen, my bad that I haven't been available, but I've been busy with moms and all of the shit in the streets," Rich told her.

"Sounds to me like you've taken the role of your brother," she replied.

"I just want niggas to feel Don's presence. I'ont want niggas to get the idea that since Don's gone, he's forgotten."

"Rich, I respect that and all, but aren't you worried about receiving the same fate as Don?" Concern arose within her tone.

"Now you're startin' to sound like my ma." He sounded annoyed. "Like I told her, I only expect you to respect the game. Besides, I'ma take out the niggas who got at you and Don."

Shanta had a flashback of that horrific night and quickly shook it away. "I wish I could tell you more about that night. At least how one of them niggas look," she sighed.

"Don't worry. I found out who one of the niggas is."

"Really? Is it anyone that we know?"

"No one that I know. It's some nigga named Ro—" Rich's iPhone chimed, cutting him off. He saw the text message was from T-Mac and read it. While he was reading the message, Shanta noticed that his facial expression became grim.

"Is everything okay, Rich?" she cared to know.

"Look, I gotta go and tend to somethin'," was all he offered.

"It's about Don, isn't it?" Shanta knew his answer from the look in his eyes. She planted a hand on his arm and said, "Your brother's problems are your own." Rich knew exactly what Shan meant, and he would do anything to solve their problems—starting by solving Don's murder in the streets.

Rich hurried out of the apartment, leaving Shanta alone with the Chinese food and her thoughts. She couldn't help but wonder who had been the ones to shoot her and murder Don. Whomever it was, she hoped Rich would make them pay with their lives. Even though she didn't know who it was, her heart was cold towards them. And if ever she found out, then...

Receiving a text on her iPhone interrupted her thoughts. Shan grabbed her phone from the side table and saw the message was from Rob. Her heart instantly warmed. Shanta couldn't help but get the feeling that Rob was bad for her. However, he made her feel so damn good.

•••

As the gang of jack-boys turned into the lot of the gas station, the four pulled down their ski masks. Their mark, Dior, was oblivious to the gang tailing her ever since she had left the beauty salon. They observed as she pulled her silver Mercedes sedan beside a gas pump, then stepped out of the vehicle and headed inside the station. A moment later, Dior returned to her ride, where she pumped gas into the tank. Before she knew it, there was a masked gunman vastly in approach with his barrel trained on her dome.

Whack!

Rob struck Dior across her face with his FN, splitting her brow. "Bitch, move it now!"

Without putting up a fight, Dior entered the backseat of the Lexus SUV. She knew the kidnappers were dead serious, seeing that they were masked up. TJ peeled outta the lot while Max, who rode shotgun, scanned the surroundings for any eyewitnesses while Rob and Bone sat on either side of the mark. The gang snatched Dior's ass up in the afternoon while she was stopped at a local gas station. She had found herself on their radar after they learned she was a major weed distributor. Actually, she was one of Trina's clients at the hair salon that Trina had put Rob onto.

"Listen, you're gonna take us to the money, or else," Rob demanded, grabbing a fistful of Dior's newly done sewn-in bundles of hair and stuffed the barrel of the FN to her jaw.

"O-okay! Just please don't kill me. I-I have kids!" Dior cried.

"As long as you don't try no funny shit, then I'll let you live to see your kids again."

"You don't have to worry." She gave up the directions to her place.

Once they arrived at the destination, Rob had yanked Dior outta the SUV and walked her inside the place with his gun pressed to her back. The rest of the gang followed closely behind. After the others searched the home, they found no one else there. Dior showed Rob to the stash spot, which was down in the basement inside of the washing machine. As TJ and Max were upstairs on lookout, Bone tossed the stash of stacks of money and individually packaged pounds of weed into a duffel bag he had brought along, while Rob made Dior lie face down and held her at gunpoint. Once the stash was collected, the gang hurried out.

•••

After hittin' the lick, Rob and the gang were in a room of the Diamond Inn hotel. TJ and Max divided the money while Bone weighed up the weed as Rob rolled up a blunt of the weed they had taken. They all sat around the table. It was another caper done for the gang, but it wasn't the one that would change their lives. Rob still had that one lined up.

Now that there was a bounty on Rob's head, he knew that he had to use his head before a nigga knocked it off his shoulders. So lately, he had been very vigilant, being sure to keep his head on the swivel and his pole ready for action. He had to admit that it bothered him knowing that at any given moment, a nigga could attempt to collect the bounty on him. So, he had to kill Rich asap in order to remove the price tag on his head.

"Listen up," Rob started, commanding the others' attention. "I've been thinkin' about the nigga Rich and his price tag.

I wanna find out that nigga whereabouts ASAP, so I can put an end to that."

Bone chuckled. "Rob, don't tell me that nigga got you scared in these streets."

"Nigga, I ain't never scared. But I ain't stupid either," he replied firmly. "It's smart for me to get rid of Rich in order to keep niggas from comin' for my head."

"Let 'em come. They'll be the ones to catch a bullet to the head instead," Bone remarked.

Rob scoffed. "Easy for you to say when you ain't the one walkin' around with money on your fuckin' head, Bone!"

"Rob's right. Killin' Rich as soon as possible would be best," TJ intervened.

"How are we gonna find him?" Max wanted to know.

"We get Swindle to tell us," Rob suggested.

"And why in hell would Swindle do that?" Bone asked. He was the only one who knew that Swindle had it out for Rob also.

"Because I still have Swindle's chain as an incentive. And if he wants it back, then he'll tell me what I need to know." Rob knew the chain was worth at least 30 Gs itself, so he figured it was enough to cover his bounty with Swindle and motivate him to give up Rich.

"I think it's worth us tryin' to get some info outta Swindle on Rich. For now, let's focus on dividin' this money in front of us," said TJ.

Rob sparked up the blunt and took a pull of it. He thought it would be best to tell the crew about the money in the grave. "Speakin' of money, just in case a nigga kills me in these streets, I want y'all to know somethin'..."

"What is it, Rob?" TJ urged. He noticed Rob was having trouble saying whatever was on his mind.

"For a few years now, I've been stashin' away money after every lick. It's buried beneath the biggest tree in the Oak Creek graveyard," he revealed.

"Why are you tellin' us this now, Rob?" TJ asked.

"'Cause I would want you all to divide the money."

"But we ain't gonna let no one kill you in these streets," Max assured.

Bone leaned back in his seat and smirked, "And if you do happen to get killed, then we'll see to it that you be buried where the money is."

"Just know that I'm hard to kill," Rob remarked, staring Bone dead in the eyes.

After dividing the gains from their lick, the gang loaded into the Lexus SUV and went on about their business. TJ dropped off Max and then Bone before steering to Rob's place, where he spun the block a couple of times to be sure they were not being tailed. Once clear, he pulled to the curb out front of the complex. During the commute, TJ noticed that Rob was silent. He could tell that Rob had shit on his mind.

"Listen, Rob," TJ began, breaking the silence. "Don't trip over that nigga Rich. We'll find his ass soon.

"It's not Rich who I'm more so trippin' over. It's Bone. I ain't feelin' how he came at me back at the hotel," Rob stressed.

"We both know that I'ont feel most the shit Bone does, but that's just the way he is, so don't trip. Whatever ill feelings you got towards him will have to be put aside so we can all be on the same wave when we hit the lick you got lined up."

"You're right. But it doesn't mean I'ma forget the remarks made by Bone." He knew it was best for him to play Bone close.

"I'ont blame you."

Rob dapped up TJ before stepping outta the Lex' and then entered the complex. He wondered if it was the best idea to reveal his money in the grave, even to those who he considered to be his friends. He understood that money could turn friends into enemies.

•••

"I'm tellin' you, Rich, if this nigga knows anything, then he was more than likely in on murkin' Don," T-Mac stressed.

"I'll hear the nigga out before anything," Rich told him.

The two were in the hood awaiting Tray, who claimed to have info on where to find Don's killers in exchange for the kilo bounty. Tray had managed to survive after Rob popped him up, and he wanted nothing more than to see Rob dead. The kilo was just a plus. Tray had sent word looking to meet with Rich. Rich didn't know who the fuck Tray was, and T-Mac tried convincing him that this nigga had it coming. But before anything, Rich wanted to at least hear Tray out in hopes of finding Don's killers.

A ragged burgundy sedan turned into the alley, its headlights illuminating the dim-lit alleyway. The sedan pulled to a stop, and as Tray stepped out, T-Mac went to draw the pole from his waist until Rich gestured for him to stand down. Seeing that Tray had come alone, Rich didn't want to alarm him before getting some answers about Don's killers.

"So, what can you tell me about the nigga Rob?" Rich pressed.

"First, hand over the paper, and then I'll tell you what I know," BD told him.

Rich nodded his head at T-Mac, who then pulled out stacks of cash wrapped with rubber bands and shoved the stacks into Tray's chest while eyeing him sharply. Tray thumbed through the stack of bills, satisfied that it all looked to be there.

"A'ight, you have the damn paper. Now, tell me what you know," Rich demanded, losing his patience.

"Look dawg, all I know is Rob, and his gang be hangin' out on 37th and Center Street. The nigga pushes a black Challenger Hellcat," Tray informed.

"And how do you know any of this shit?"

"I know Rob from around the way."

"Nigga, why should we fuckin' believe you? How we don't know if this is a lie to collect the bounty or a setup?" T-Mac piped in with his temper flarin'.

"If I'm lyin', then I'm dyin'," Tray replied.

Rich pulled the FN from his waist and then stuffed its barrel to Tray's stomach. "Then let's hope you won't be dyin' in vain."

Bluke, bluke, bluke!

The muffled shots Tray took were fatal, and his body crumpled onto the pavement. Rich thought it was best to off him being that if there was any truth to what the nigga told him, he didn't want Tray living to tell the story. Rich didn't know who Rob was, but he would be sure to do his research. And if what Tray had told him was true, then Rich would be sure Tray didn't die in vain because he would definitely gun after Rob with a vengeance.

As Rich stepped into his whip before following suit, T-Mac picked up the stack of money, which was now splattered with blood.

CHAPTER 12

Shanta made her way to the front door of Angie's home. It had been a few weeks since they last spoke, and Shanta felt the need to stop by and see how Angie was holding up. As hard as it was on Shanta losing Don, she was sure it had to be even harder on Angie, being that he was her son. Therefore, she wanted Angie to know that she was there for her.

It was afternoon when Shanta showed up at Angie's place, and she knew Angie was present, seeing that her Jaguar was still parked in the driveway. Before ringing the doorbell, Shan took a deep breath. She hoped that Angie would be happy to see her. A moment later, Angie slowly pulled open the door and seemed surprised to find Shan there.

"Hey Angie," Shanta greeted with a smile.

"Shan? What are you doing here?" Angie wasn't expecting her, and quite frankly, she didn't care for any company right then.

"Just thought that I should see how you're holding up. Mind if I come in?"

Angie hesitated before stepping aside. "Y-yes, come on in."

Once Shanta entered the home, she immediately noticed that it was untidy, unlike usual. And she couldn't help but notice that Angie was unkempt. Shan credited it to Angie still grieving over Don's death, and partially she was correct. But little did she know, Angie was back on crack, and Angie wanted to keep her relapse a secret because she knew that Shan would inform Rich. Also, she was embarrassed by it and didn't want or need anyone disappointed in her.

The two made their way into the front room and sat on the couch. The last time Shanta had been to Angie's home was during the get-together following Don's burial. She actually missed the Sunday dinners they used to have there, and nothing seemed the same now that Don was gone.

"So, how have you been?" Shan wanted to know.

Angie sighed. "I've just been trying not to grieve so much over Don, but it's easier said than done."

"I know what you mean. So far, there has not been a day that I haven't thought about him since his death. However, we have to find the strength within us to live on. It's what he would want."

"Sounds like something Rich would say."

"Well, Rich did tell me something similar. By the way, how has he been?"

"Not himself. He feels like he has to fill the place of Don in the streets. And I'm afraid that I'll lose him too if he doesn't change his ways," Angie stressed.

"Listen, Rich may be stuck in his ways, but the street life is all he and Don have known."

"Maybe you should talk with Rich before he ends up losing his life in those streets."

"I can't promise you any changes, but I'll talk with him," Shanta told her. She had an idea. "Why don't you have us all over for Sunday dinner? That way, Rich and I will be able to talk without distractions. It's been a while since you've had us over here for dinner anyway. Why is that?"

"Because I just haven't been in the mood for cooking. Besides, without Don here, I don't want the dinner to seem like it's missing something. So, I don't think that's a good idea." Partially that was true, but Angie failed to mention that she wasn't in the mood to cook because lately, she was high on crack.

Shanta studied her a moment. She noticed there was something different about Angie but couldn't pinpoint exactly what. "Angie, are you sure there's nothing else going on with you? Because if theirs is, then feel free to let me know."

"Look, I already told you that I'm still grieving. I don't need you here trying to make something else out of the situation, Shanta," Angie snapped.

"I didn't mean to come here and upset you, Angie. I just want you to know that I'm here for you," Shan said. She stood from the couch. "I'll leave you be. Get in touch with me if you ever need me for anything." Shan showed herself to the door.

It was Angie's guilt of relapsing which made her so defensive. Part of her wanted to tell Shanta in the hopes of getting some help battling her addiction, but she didn't want Shan to look at her as if Don's help wasn't already enough. So, Angie was left to get clean on her own. And all of the pressure had her wanting to get high.

•••

"Ladies first."

"How sweet!"

Pulling the door open, Rich allowed Brittany to enter the boutique first. It was a cute little spot that sold high-end women's fashion, and Rich had brought Brittany there to splurge on her. Rich felt that he had been neglecting her lately with all that was going down in the streets, so he just wanted to do something nice for his girl. And Brittany was excited because she looked forward to him spending time with her more than anything. Thus far, their relationship was getting better with each day, and they enjoyed each other.

As the couple browsed around, Rich helped Brittany pick out a few things that he thought would look good on her. Brittany was like a kid in a candy store, and she had good taste. After picking out a selection of clothes, Brittany coaxed Rich over to the dressing rooms, where she would try on the clothes and model them for him. Though Rich had been the one to bring Brittany to the boutique, getting to watch her model clothes was his reward. He was always excited to take her out and show her off. Surprisingly, Kat emerged from one of the dressing rooms, where she had tried on a few outfits. She and the others immediately took notice to each other. Disregarding Brittany, Kat approached Rich and gave him a lingering hug.

"You're looking good as usual," Kat smiled, all up in his personal space. "How have you been?"

"Been chasin' a bag," Rich answered, keeping it simple.

"Looks to me like you're about to blow a bag today." Kat noticed the pile of clothes they had picked out.

"I'ont mind blowin' a bag on my girl. By the way, have you met Brittany here?"

Brittany stepped beside Rich, wrapping her arm around his waist as to claim her man, and said, "Yes, Kat and I met briefly once before. I think she's... nice."

"Well, you thought wrong, boo-boo, because if anything, I'm a bad bitch," Kat replied with a hint of attitude. "Anywho," she returned her attention to Rich. "If ever you want to talk, then slide in my DM."

"Kat, I ain't one of those niggas who follow you on social media," Rich told her.

"Then maybe you should, because I'm sure you'd like my pics," Kat purred. She rested the attire she didn't want on top of the pile of clothes that Brittany was to try on. "Those are too basic for me, so I'm sure they're perfect for your girl." With no further words, Kat strutted away to make her purchase before exiting the boutique.

Brittany knew that Kat was throwing shade. "That hoe has some nerves coming for me like that."

"Listen, Britt," Rich pulled her close, "Kat don't have nothin' on you, so don't let her make you insecure."

"Insecure? Boy, please!" Britt scoffed. "If anything, she makes me irritated. Hoes like her always believe they can take any man. I see how she was coming on to you."

"Kat or no girl can ever take me from you," Rich assured.

"That's how it better be unless you want me to fuck you up," she half-joked.

"I ain't tryna get fucked up," he chuckled.

"Hope not." Britt grabbed up a romper from the pile of clothes. "Now, you wait here while I try on this and show the hoe Kat how to make something basic look boujee," she told him. One thing Rich loved about her is that she kept it basic but boujee. Britt pecked Rich's lips before entering the dressing room, leaving him waiting in anticipation. Nevertheless, Rich knew that she was worth the wait.

•••

Shanta and Kat showed up at the dinner party that Parker put together at Castle's place. After parking the car, Shanta and Kat stepped out and then approached the huge home. The girls had to admit that they were impressed with how Castle was living large. Parker was always sure to speak of it. Once Shan chimed the doorbell, a moment later, Parker answered and was happy to see her girls.

"Glad you came," Parker greeted her girls and offered them both hugs.

"You know we had to come for you, girl," Shanta replied.

"And we damn sure wasn't going to miss the opportunity to finally meet Castle," Kat added.

Parker stepped aside and allowed Shanta and Kat to enter the astonishing home. There were others in attendance who were all mingling and enjoying themselves. The dinner party was nothing fancy, it was more so casual, and the girls seemed to fit right in with the party. Parker led her girls to the living room, where they approached Castle.

"Baby, these are my girls that I told you all about, Shanta and Kat," Parker introduced them. "And girls, this is Castle, my—"

"Close friend," Castle intervened. He gently shook both girls' hands. "Parker told me all about you."

"Well, she barely told us anything about you," Shanta said.

"Besides how fine and rich you are," Kat added.

"At least I know she bragged about me," Castle smiled.

Parker slipped an arm around his waist. "All you need to know is Castle's a good nigga."

Castle led the girls over to the mini bar, where he poured them each a drink of their choice. He wanted Parker and her girls to have a good time. It was obvious to him that Parker thought of herself as his bitch, but Castle didn't think of it that way. If you asked him, Parker was just another one of his bitches that he used as a roadrunner. He didn't have the same feelings for her as she did for him. For Castle, it was nothing personal, just business. However, Parker seemed to be mixing pleasure with business.

One of Castle's boys approached him. "Yo Castle, I'ont mean to interrupt, but there's some trouble with the last load."

"Trouble like what?" Castle asked.

"Like five keys short."

Castle looked to Parker and asked, "Did you notice the load was short?"

"No, I didn't."

"Go and call the connect," Castle told his boy, who then stepped away. He returned his attention to the girls.

"Look, I got some business to tend to. Nice to meet you, ladies." Castle pecked Parker's lips before heading for the den, where his boys and load of drugs were.

Shanta had an idea that Castle was a drug dealer, and now it was confirmed. "Parker, why didn't you mention to us that you are involved with Castle's drug ring?"

"Why would you keep something like that away from us?" Kat input.

"I just didn't want either of you to be worried about me," Parker responded.

"As your girls, we're supposed to be worried about you," replied Shan.

Parker sipped at her drink. "Well, don't be because I know what I'm doing. Now, how about we enjoy ourselves."

Not wanting to ruin the dinner party, Shanta decided not to press Parker any further about what she was into, but it wasn't the last Shanta would bring it up. She just didn't want Parker to find herself in harm's way on behalf of Castle. After being with Don, she knew it was possible to become collateral damage.

Martell "Troublesome" Bolden

CHAPTER 13

Shanta looked herself over in the full-length mirror. She thought that she looked good from head to toe. Her hair was in soft curls, makeup light, and her accessories were only diamond hoop earrings along with her lady Rolex. And her curves were on display in her white blouse and floral print pencil skirt, plus the white Prada slingback stilettos she wore matched her handbag. She wanted to keep it cute for her date tonight.

The doorbell chimed. Shanta gave herself one final once over in the mirror before heading to answer the front door. Pulling open the door, she found Rob standing there wearing a winning smile. Damn, he's looking good, she mused, seeing him with a fresh haircut, diamond earrings, and a Rolex on his wrist. He sported a green and black Gucci polo shirt with black stonewashed jeans and Gucci Loafers. Overall, Rob was dressed to impress.

"Hey you," Shanta greeted him. The two embraced, her arms around the nape of his neck and his hands on the small of her back.

"C'mon, so I can take you out and show you off," Rob said and grabbed her by the hand, leading her towards his whip.

They entered Rob's Hellcat and then set off on their way. Rob liked being in the company of Shanta. She was his type. Not only was she a bad bitch, but she was a good girl. He just didn't want to rush things with her. Shan was into Rob, although part of her felt like she was moving on too fast. It had been only a month since she and he met. Shanta found comfort in Rob, but she wasn't quite ready to completely open up to him just yet, especially not about Don.

Arriving at the destination downtown, Rob parked the whip before Benihana. He stepped out and opened the passenger door for Shanta, and then the couple entered the up-scale restaurant, where the host seated them at an intimate table for two. The atmosphere was dimly lit and decorated lavishly, fitting for wining and dining. Shortly thereafter, a waitress materialized to take Rob and Shanta's orders, and Rob ordered them both steak and asparagus with a glass of Moscato, then the waitress bustled away.

Leaning back in his chair, Rob fixated his gaze on Shanta. "Mind if I ask you somethin'?"

"No, I don't mind," Shanta replied.

"What's a girl as bad as you doin' single?" he wanted to know.

Shanta took a brief moment before responding. "I just didn't want to rush right into anything after my recent relationship."

"Well, just know that I ain't rushin' to love, so we can take things nice and slow. I just wanna know you better. For starters, what do you want in a man?" He smiled charmingly.

Ideally, what Shanta wanted was for a man to be like Don. However, she knew that she had to eventually move on and get to know a man for who he is. She said, "I just want a man who's sure of himself. And how about you? What do you want in a woman?"

"I want a woman who knows her worth." He understood that a woman who knew her worth isn't willing to settle for less.

"Aww, that's sweet."

"That's real."

The waitress returned with their meals and drinks. Over their meals, they enjoyed each other's conversation and shared some laughs. Their personalities were compatible, Rob adored that she was reserved, and Shanta admired that he was a flirt. Things couldn't be going any better between them.

Following their dinner, they were back in traffic while smoking on a blunt filled with za as music played in the background. Shanta glanced over at Rob. She thought he was definitely a fine-ass nigga. However, she didn't want to seem desperate or give him the wrong impression. Glancing over at Shanta, Rob caught her looking him over.

"Look but don't touch." Rob smiled.

"Boy, shut up and drive," Shan chuckled. Once Summer Walker's "Girls Need Love Too" played into the music rotation, she exclaimed, "Ooh, this is my song!" She began singing along with the lyrics. Rob shook his head. "Don't quit your day job, whatever that is."

Shanta playfully pushed him. "Whatevs! And FYI, actually, I don't have a job because I own a boutique."

"Good for you. I admire a bitch who's about her coins."

"Just out of curiosity, do you have a job or what?" she probed. He glanced over at her and said, "Let's just say my job is stayin' alive."

"I take it that you get it how you live."

"I ain't proud of the way I live, but it's how a nigga survives. So, please don't judge me, and I won't judge you."

She shifted towards him in her seat. "And I don't judge you at all. I just hope that you can see a life outside of the way you're currently living."

This made Rob think about TJ being done with the stickup game after their next big lick. Rob did have more than enough money in the grave stashed away to invest into going legit also. Honestly, he didn't want hittin' licks to be his livelihood, even if there would always be marks who are sweet. Ultimately, he knew that sooner or later, it was bound to catch up to him. Now knowing that Rich had a price tag on his head for murkin' Don was proof of that. Only if Rob knew that Shanta had been dramatically affected by the life he lived.

Subsequent to leaving the restaurant, Rob pulled the Hellcat to the curb before Shanta's place, which she had once shared with Don. He stepped out the whip, opened the passenger door for her, and then walked her up to the front door of her home.

"I enjoyed kickin' it with you today," Shan said, all smiles.

"I'm just glad that you came," Rob replied.

"Admittedly, I mainly came because my girls practically made me. But I'm glad they did."

"Maybe you'll let me take you out again sometime."

"Only if you promise not to take me out to some fancy-ass restaurant next time. I don't know what you take me as but, I ain't some bougie bitch," she half-joked.

"Promise next time I'll take you someplace chill."

"I'd like that." Shanta hesitantly pecked him on the corner of his lips and then turned for her place.

He grabbed her wrist, stopping her. "You never told me what happened with your last relationship. I mean, how it ended."

Shan peered off down the street. "It ended when the man I was with was robbed and killed. And it happened right in front of me while I was in the car. One of the robbers also shot me."

Rob couldn't believe what he was hearing. Of all people, Shanta turned out to be the girl who was with Don the night of the lick who Rob had shot. Apparently, she didn't know he had anything to do with Don being murked and that he was actually the one who had shot her. At that moment, Rob didn't know what to think or how to feel. His mind was telling him that he needed to leave her be, but his heart wanted her to be his.

"Look, sorry about what happened to you," Rob said in a lowered voice, with a guilty conscience.

Shan turned and looked into his eyes. "Don't be sorry because it's not your fault," she replied, naïve to the fact that he was more at fault than anyone. "Good night."

Rob returned to his Hellcat, pressed the push to start button, and then stabbed off. As he steered the whip eastbound, his mind was on Shan. Never did he ever expect to be in such a binding position. Not only did he have a hand in murkin' her lover, Don, he also meant to murk her. He knew that he couldn't tell her about being involved in what happened that night. However, if she happened to find out, then what? Rob wanted Shanta more than he thought, even if that meant being dangerously in love.

Meanwhile, inside the loft, Shanta kicked off her heels near the front door and sat her Prada bag on the end table as she stepped into the front room. Making her way through the master bedroom and into the adjacent bathroom, she turned on the water in the shower. After collecting her bathing essentials, she stepped inside the walk-in shower, and as the warm water cascaded over her, she couldn't help but think about her date with Rob.

There was no denying that she liked Rob. He treated her nicely and made her feel good. Not to mention, she thought the nigga was fine as hell. She never expected to meet someone so soon who could make her like him as much as she did Don. There was still a part of her that didn't want to move on from Don too soon. But she knew Don would care for her to be happy, and if Rob could do that for her, then she was sure Don would approve. If only she knew better. No matter what, *I'll never stop loving you, Don*, she mused.

Following her shower, Shanta pulled on a pair of PJs. She was seated in front of the vanity mirror in her bedroom, wrapping her hair in a silk scarf, when her iPhone chimed, indicating an incoming text message. Seeing the text was from Kat, she pressed the touchscreen and read the message.

KAT:
How's ur date? Hope u ain't doing nothing I wouldn't do...
Shanta chuckled as she shook her head at how fast her girl is.

Shanta sent her a text in reply.

SHAN:
Actually, the date is over. But it was nice.

KAT:
Bitch, sounds to me like u didn't smash. SMDH...

SHAN:
When have I ever been the kind of bitch to let a nigga smash on the first date? I ain't u. LBVS.

KAT:
Damn right u ain't me, becuz I woulda had his ass in my bed sleeping like a baby!

SHAN:
Hoe, u so cray. LOL. Why don't u stop focusing on who's in my bed becuz I'm sure there's someone in urs. Besides, I rather take it nice n slow w/ Rob. I really do like him. I just don't wanna feel like I'm moving on too fast from Don.

KAT:
Don will always be in ur heart, although u still have room

for someone else. And just maybe that someone is Rob.

SHAN:
U right. Thnx for being here for me. I <3 u.

KAT:
Bitch, u already know that I <3 u too. And FYI, someone is in my bed right now, and I'm about to rock him to sleep. TTYL.

"Kat's ass is something else," Shanta thought aloud as she chuckled. She had to admit that Kat was right about Rob. Maybe he was the one for her now that she no longer had Don. Looking over at the photo of her and Don on the nightstand, it was hard for her to think about how she and Don were supposed to be married with children, yet someone took that away from her. If only she knew that, of all people, that someone was actually the nigga she thought maybe the one for her, Rob.

•••

In the front room of TJ's place, he and Rob sat on the couch, sharing a blunt while playing NBA2K on Xbox. They needed to just chill after hittin' their last lick and take some to prepare for the lick on Castle. Plus, with the bounty out on them, Rob had advised the gang to lay low for a few days. The less they were visible, the more they were allusive from Twelve and opps.

TJ hit the blunt once more before passing it to his boy. "You might as well pay me now because this game is over," he said, referring to their friendly wager on the game.

"Nigga, there's still several seconds on the shot clock, and my team has the ball," Rob replied. He played with the Milwaukee Bucks.

"We'll see."

"He shoots. He scores!" Rob jumped to his feet excitedly after sinking the game-winning shot at the buzzer. "See, you should never count out Giannis. Now, pay up!"

TJ chuckled as he handed over the winnings. "That's just luck."

"If anything, I'm lucky to be alive," Rob responded in all seriousness. He sat back on the couch and placed the joystick on the coffee table.

"Yeah, because it seems like death is around every corner." TJ placed his controller on the coffee table also and then shifted towards his boy. "Look, I think it's best that once we hit this major lick, you got lined up, you should retire from the stick-up game. With the money you already have buried away, you could flip the game," he suggested.

Rob hit the blunt. "Between you and me, that's my plan. You better believe I'ont wanna be strippin' niggas for the rest of my life. I wanna get out before it's too late. But keep this between us for now because I'ont know how Bone and Max are gonna take it." He understood that, unlike the others, TJ was reasonable, so he could talk with him about anything. Not to mention he and TJ were each other's right-hand men.

TJ scoffed. "Who gives a fuck about what Bone or Max thinks. If them niggas wanna continue to rob for a livin', then that's on them. Mainly Bone, he just doesn't seem to get it."

"Maybe you and Bone need to have a talk because I ain't pickin' sides."

"If that's what he wants, then I'm down."

"Good. Because I need both of you on the same page when we hit that major lick, I'll get with you tomorrow," Rob told him and stood to his feet. His iPhone chimed, and he noticed it was a text from Shanta. "It's Shanta."

"Apparently, you two have gotten really close," TJ probed.

"She's a good bitch, and I like spendin' time with her."

"Sounds like she's a keeper."

Rob puffed the blunt of za before passing it to his boy. "Fa sho. Look, I gotta get goin'."

"Rob," TJ rose to his feet, "you think it's a good idea to be out in those streets with the bounty out on you behind that nigga Don?"

"About that..." He felt the need to tell TJ exactly who Shanta was.

"What about it, Rob?"

"Shanta. She is the girl that was there the night we murked Don," Rob revealed.

"So, you mean to tell me that she's the girl that you shot that night?"

"Right. And get this, she was in love with Don."

"And now she's fallin' in love with you..." TJ's voice faded.

"Believe me, it's always on my conscience whenever I'm with Shanta," he admitted.

"I'm sure it is. How did you find out that she was the one there?"

"Durin' an in-depth discussion about our past relationships is when she described how she lost Don, and then I immediately knew."

TJ met his eyes. "Does she know?"

"No, she doesn't know that I had anything to do with what happened that night."

"Rob, maybe you should forget about this girl before things become more complicated than they already are," TJ suggested.

Rob sighed. "Look, I get what you're sayin', TJ. But it's not easy for me to just forget about her. You know how it is to feel for a girl that maybe you shouldn't," he replied. "I'll get with you tomorrow. And don't worry, this Glock will keep me safe in those streets."

Without further words, Rob made an exit, and TJ locked the door behind him. Making his way back to the couch, TJ took a seat and then puffed the blunt. He did know exactly how it is to feel for a girl that maybe he shouldn't, given his own relationship with Kayla. *I just hope Rob knows what he's gettin' himself into*, he contemplated.

CHAPTER 14

C-note was in the trap spot, finishing bagging up some work. Afterward, he would distribute it to the rest of the spots. It being a Friday, he wanted to distribute the work ASAP because he knew it was a payday. Once that business was taken care of, he and the others would hit up the club later tonight.

After the work was bagged up, C-note tossed it inside a Fendi backpack and then made his way outside onto the front porch. He looked up and down the street, finding the block was quiet in the night. *Danger shoulda been had his ass here by now*, he thought and was a bit annoyed by the tardiness. Pulling out his iPhone, he dialed Danger, who was supposed to come pick him up in order to escort him to make the last drop-offs/pickups for the night at the other trap spots. As the line rang, C-note heard the bushes in front of the trap rustle, and once a nigga jumped out with a gun in hand, who was rockin' all black, C-note knew the nigga was there to murk him. Instantaneously C-note dropped his phone as he reached for his waist, going for his own gun...

Boc, boc, boc, boc, boc!

The gunfire crackled in the night, and C-note dropped onto the porch steps after catching three gunshots, two in the chest and one in the neck. He chased his breath as the nigga stepped up over C-note, aiming down on him, and then fired a couple more shots into C-note's chest. The nigga then pried the backpack from C-note's hand and hurried away like a thief in the night.

Just as Danger had answered C-note's call, he overheard the sound of rapid gunshots. He didn't exactly know what had taken place, but he feared the worse. Shortly thereafter, Danger sped his Chevy Donk down the block, bringing it to a screeching halt in the middle of the street before the trap spot.

Pushing the door open, he hopped out the whip with his Glock in hand and looked around for anything amiss as he ran over to C-note, who was barely clinging on to life.

"Stay with me, C-note! Who did this shit to you?" Danger was heated as hell at the sight of his boy on the brink of death. If he found out who had hit up C-note, then he would catch a body.

C-note couldn't muster enough strength to speak. Even if he could, then he wouldn't be able to tell Danger who had popped him, being that he didn't see the nigga's face. At least if he was gonna die, he would have preferred the nigga to look him dead in the eyes before taking him out. That way, he could hunt the nigga for the rest of his days. C-note's breaths became labored, and right before Danger's eyes, he changed over.

•••

"Did you get the nigga?" Swindle asked eagerly.

"Rich wasn't even there, but I did get one of his boys," Bone reported and then sipped at his bottle of Budweiser.

"Shit." Swindle slammed his fist down on the bar top out of frustration.

The two met at the poolhall, where they sat at the bar having drinks. Swindle was meeting with Bone about the hit on Rich and to make sure their next move was their best move. He had attempted to set up Rich for Bone to rob and kill, just as he did Don. However, he didn't anticipate Rich to be missing in action.

"Did you at least get some work?" Swindle wanted to know.

Bone sat the Fendi backpack in Swindle's lap. "Here's at least a half key. It's yours for ten Gs," he bargained.

"Cool," Swindle agreed. He took a swig from his glass of Remy. "I can't have that nigga Rich alive because he's bound to find out that I was behind his boys bein' murked."

"Who gives a fuck if he finds out? The nigga is a dead man walkin' any-fuckin'-way," Bone replied nonchalantly.

"The sooner he's dead, the better off my drug operation is. If he finds out I had parts in you murkin' his boys, then he'll want beef, and that'll get in the way of me bein' able to move product. I can't beef and get money. And I ain't gonna let no nigga get in the way of my hustle. Feel me?"

"Yeah, I feel you, dawg." Bone sipped his drink.

"Look, we gotta get rid of Rich ASAP. As long as he's still alive, then you'll have a price tag on your head, and I'll be at risk of bein' exposed of settin' up Don. We can't have him gettin' in the way of us gettin' paid."

"We'll get Rich ass out the way before he can find out anything," Bone assured. "Well, Rob wants Rich dead just as bad since he put money on Rob's head. So, I can use Rob to get the job done. He planned on comin' to you in order to get the drop on Rich."

"Is that so?"

"It is. Said he has your chain as an incentive, and he would use it to get you to tell him what he wants to know about Rich if you want your chain back."

I knew all along it was Rob who stripped me for my chain and shit, Swindle thought, seething. Nigga got me fucked up if he thinks I'ma let him get away with it. "Rob can keep the chain. But if you really wanna go into business with me for yourself, then now is your chance."

"What do you mean?" Bone inquired.

"I mean, you should burn Rob and then collect the bounty. That way, you'll get everything you want. It's a win-win," he expounded.

As much as Bone held ill feelings towards Rob, he had never considered killing him. However, he had to admit that Swindle made a good point. But Bone had to give killing Rob some real consideration. "I get what you mean, dawg, and there's a lot that I need to consider."

"Bone, the only thing you need to consider is whether or not you wanna takeover. And we don't need Heavy or Rob suspectin' us of nothin'. Them two niggas don't even know what's comin'. Let's keep it that way. I'll be in touch." Swindle polished off his drink before heading out the poolhall, leaving Bone there considering his options.

•••

Rich and T-Mac were waiting in the parking lot of a strip mall for Danger. After watching C-note die before his eyes, Danger had called them with the devastating news and told them to meet with him there instead of on the block.

"First Don, and now C-note. Can't believe this shit!" Rich breathed, aggravated.

"Whoever did this shit to C-note gotta pay for it. We can't let niggas gettin' away with gunnin' for us again," T-Mac stated.

"I feel you."

Rich and T-Mac were posted outside of their whips baring the fall weather when Danger recklessly turned his Chevy into the lot. Danger parked and hopped out, leaving his whip idling. The two saw the blood of C-note painted all over Danger's gray Blue Bands Only sweatsuit and his once all-white Air Jordan sneakers. They all wanted to make the streets bleed in retaliation.

Danger stomped over to the others and cried, "They... they got C-note."

"Calm down, Danger, and tell us what happened," Rich told him in a calming tone.

"I was runnin' late on my way to scoop him up when he called me, and next thing I hear is gunshots on the other end of the line. Once I pulled up, then I found C-note bleedin' to death. I-I couldn't do a damn thing to save him..." His words faded.

Rich and T-Mac had never before seen Danger so distraught. They could see that he had pain Danger's his eyes.

T-Mac let out a sharp breath. "Don't trip. We'll get who did this."

"Any clue who may have done this?" Rich asked.

"Maybe it was Heavy," T-Mac replied.

Danger paced back and forth. "Then how 'bout we go and snatch up Heavy's fat-ass then torture him until he talks."

"As long as we're coppin' weight from Heavy, then he has no real reason to do this. It has to be someone we don't expect, and maybe it's even whoever had somethin' to do with what happened to Don," Rich explained. He had the right idea but didn't yet know it.

"So, what should we do now?" asked T-Mac.

Rich looked to T-Mac and Danger and said, "We keep gettin' paid until we find out exactly who's behind all of this shit. Then we'll make 'em pay in blood."

•••

Heavy was parked in the alley behind one of his trap spots. He was seated in his whip, awaiting Swindle to show up. As Swindle approached the whip, he perpetually surveyed the surroundings before stepping into the passenger seat. Swindle had called Heavy there to pick up some profits. Being later in the night, the back alley was only dimly lit by the light poles.

"Don't know if you heard but, someone smoked C-note. That nigga knew what came with bein' in these streets," Heavy commented carelessly.

"Nigga, and so do you," Swindle hissed as he whipped out his Glock, then trained it on Heavy's face.

Heavy looked confused. "Fuck is this shit about, Swindle?"

"It's about me takin' shit over now."

Blam, blam!

Each .45 caliber slug ate into Heavy's face. Swindle could hear Heavy's pathetic attempt to catch his breath and then pumped one more slug into Heavy's top, causing his brain matter to splatter all over the windshield. After leaving Heavy dead, Swindle left the body there to be found.

CHAPTER 15

Crack smoke filled the atmosphere of the trap house as Angie and some other crackheads got high. Despite what a now dead Heavy had warned him before, Swindle still allowed Angie into the trap, not giving a fuck if Rich found out. He planned to get Rich out the way soon anyhow. It would be one less nigga Swindle would have to worry about getting in the way of shit.

Angie tried her best to fight her temptations, but it was difficult now that she had relapsed. She had been selling her body and renting out her vehicle in exchange for crack. She hid her relapse from Rich as best as she could because she figured that if he found out that she was back doing drugs, then it would disappoint him. Ever since losing Don, Angie turned back to smoking crack in order to cope with the loss. But she had to admit that there was a better way to go about it. Smoking crack was just the easiest way.

After receiving a phone call from Rich, Swindle had to get some product prepared in order to sell him. Even though he had it out for Rich, Swindle knew it was best to keep the nigga unaware. Including when it came to him servin' Angie, so Swindle told her ass to stay in the kitchen while he dealt with Rich. Not wanting Rich to see her cracked out, Angie agreed to stay out of sight. Shortly thereafter, Rich pulled his whip to the curb in front of the trap spot. Needing product to distribute, he was there to cop some weight. Though he had heard that Heavy was found dead a few nights ago, Rich didn't have many choices for a plug, so until he found himself another, he still had to cop work from Swindle. If only Rich knew that Swindle was the cause of a lot of his pain and grief.

"Dawg, I ain't feelin' this coppin' work shit from Swindle because I'ont trust his ass," T-Mac stressed.

"Same. But until another plug come along, he's it," Rich replied.

"I still ain't willin' to let him slide for sendin' those shooters at us."

Rich looked over at T-Mac. "Cuz, trust me, we ain't gonna let him or no niggas slide. But let's get this money for now."

Before stepping out the whip, Rich stuffed his pole on his waist, and T-Mac followed suit. They kept their guns close with all of the bodies dropping lately because neither of them wanted to be the next to be murked.

Approaching the trap spot, they were allowed inside and then led down into the basement area. Upon entering, there was Swindle seated on the couch with Vito alongside him. Swindle had forewarned Vito to play it cool, for now. He knew it would take a lot for Vito not to pop off, knowing that Rich was the nigga who pulled up on them in traffic and shot Vito and smoked Q in retaliation. As much as Swindle wanted Rich dead, there was a time and place for everything. And Swindle was definitely plotting to catch Rich at the right time and the right place to have him bodied because he knew that it was either him or Rich.

"You bring all the money?" Swindle asked and made his way towards Rich.

"It's all there," Rich replied as he handed over a bankroll. "Now, where's the product?"

"Vito, go and grab the work." Swindle thumbed through the money while Vito stepped away.

"Now that Heavy is outta the game, I guess you runnin' shit now," Rich commented. He felt that Swindle always wanted to be in charge, on the low. Swindle eyed him a moment. "Look, Heavy was a good nigga. But in this game, good niggas aren't the ones who last. It's niggas with balls that do. Feel me?"

"Any word on who tested Heavy's balls?"

"No word yet," Swindle deceived. He would never reveal the truth of his betrayal. "What about you, anything on who hit up C-note?"

"Nothin'. But you better believe we won't stop til we dead every nigga that have it out for us," Rich swore.

"Just know that niggas are out for blood. It's crazy how both Heavy and C-note were made examples of that on the same night." Rich held Swindle's eyes. "Don't know about you but, we lost a good friend in C-note that night."

"Well, Heavy was just a business partner. So I'ont take losin' him personal," Swindle stated.

Vito returned with three individually packaged bricks and tossed them atop the pool table. Picking up the bricks, T-Mac examined them to make sure it was good quality cocaine. There was a lot of tension in the air. T-Mac noticed Vito mean-mugging and clutching the pole on his waist, so T-Mac shot him a mug in return. If only T-Mac or Rich was aware that Vito had been one of the hitters who fanned out the trap spot the night, T-Mac was shot. To be aware is to be alive.

"You got what you came for," Swindle said.

"Maybe next time I'll come for more," Rich told him, offering a subliminal threat. He turned and headed out the trap with T-Mac closely behind. Vito looked over at Swindle and stated, "I wanna put a slug in that nigga, Rich. And T-Mac can get it too."

"You'll get another chance to, trust."

"Wish me and Q woulda smoked them bitch-ass niggas the first time we had the chance."

Swindle patted Vito's shoulder and responded, "We'll get payback for Q."

Making his way upstairs into the kitchen, Swindle found Angie seated at the table smoking crack. There was a quarter brick of Swindle's dope sitting out on the table, and he immediately noticed that it had been tampered with. Apparently, someone had stolen a chunk of the dope, and the only person around was Angie.

Swindle drew his pistol and slapped Angie with it several times across her face, then he barked, "Bitch, you must be crazy, thinkin' you could get away with stealin' from me!"

"I-I'm sorry, Swindle! I'll pay you back!" Angie cried out. Her lower lip was bloodied, and her right eye was blackened.

"Shut the fuck up and get the hell out, now!" Swindle snatched up Angie by a fistful of her hair and then forced her to the door, where he shoved her outside. "Bitch, if I catch your ass around here again, then I'll make sure you end up dead like I did Don!" he threatened before slamming the door shut in her face.

Angie couldn't believe what she had just heard. She never expected that Swindle had anything to do with Don's murder, and now Angie wished more than anything that she never allowed Swindle to lure her back in with the manipulation of drugs. Apparently, Swindle had a hidden agenda the entire time, and she felt like she had let her sons down. However, Angie knew that Swindle had to get what he had coming.

•••

There was a knock at the front door of Shanta's place. She was expecting company, so she knew it was none other than Rob. They had scheduled a date night since it had been a few days since they'd seen one another. And Shan was excited that Rob was coming through to chill with her.

"Coming," Shanta called out as she checked her glamour once again in the vanity mirror in her bedroom to be sure she was looking flawless. Her hair was pulled back into a ponytail, and she wore only lip gloss. The white crop top and biker shorts she wore displayed her figure, and her open-toe Gucci slides showed off her pedicure that matched her manicure. She was dressed comfortably while keeping it cute.

Approaching the door, Shanta pulled it open and found Rob there, displaying his irresistible smile. "S'up, boo," he said, rubbing his palms. She thought he was looking good with his fresh haircut. He was wearing a royal blue Nike sweatsuit that had a large white Nike checkmark stretching across the chest, a pair of crisp white Air Force Ones, and the only jewels he rocked were the diamond earrings and Rolly.

"Hey," Shanta greeted Rob and offered him a hug.

"You look good, boo," Rob complimented Shan as he admired her from head to toe.

"I know, right!"

Shanta stepped aside and allowed Rob inside, then locked the door behind him. He kicked off his tennis shoes near the front door before following her into the front room, where he took a seat on the couch. Rob was looking forward to spending time with Shan tonight.

"Smells good in here," Rob commented, smelling the aroma of homemade popcorn wafting from the kitchen. "Hope you don't burn the popcorn." He grabbed up the remote, then kicked his feet up onto the glass coffee table, and Shan pushed his feet right back down onto the floor.

"Boy, you're gonna eat the popcorn no matter what. Find us something good to watch. I'll be right back."

Shanta headed for the kitchen, and Rob admired her ass in the biker shorts. He sat back on the couch, searching for something to watch on Netflix while she went to prep the popcorn. A moment later, Shan returned with a huge bowl of buttered popcorn and sat it on the coffee table, then took a seat beside Rob on the couch. Rob put on The Hate U Give while they shared the bowl of popcorn.

"Apparently, you know how to make popcorn, but what else can you make?" Rob asked.

"Reservations," Shan half-joked.

Rob playfully tossed a few puffs of the popcorn at her and chuckled. "A home-cooked meal is good and all, but I'ont mind eatin' out," he offered an innuendo and licked his butter-covered lips.

"I'm sure you don't." She blushed.

"Rob, what is it about me that you're into? Because if all you want from me is sex, then—"

"Sex ain't better than love, Shan," he intervened. "I'm into to you 'cause you're able to bring the best outta me. Whenever I'm with you, I feel like I'ont deserve you. Although I'm grateful to have you."

Shanta shifted towards him. "So, you love me?"

"Yeah, I do."

"Listen, to be real with you. I never thought that I would ever be able to love another man after Don was taken away from me. But I do love you too, Rob."

Hearing Shanta mention Don being taken away from her weighed heavy on Rob's heart. He cared about her so much that it tore him up to know that he had actually been the one to take Don away from her, yet selfishly he cared to have her all to himself, even if that meant him having to be the one who had taken out Don. Then again, part of him felt the need to admit it to her with the hopes that she loved him enough to forgive him. Although he knew it was a thin line between love and hate.

"Shan," Rob began in close to a whisper, "I wanna talk to you about Don—"

Shanta leaned over and kissed his lips. "Let's not talk about Don right now," she told him and then commenced kissing him passionately. In that moment, she just wanted to focus on moving forward with Rob, especially after grieving over Don for so long. It felt so good to have a man's hands all over her again, and Rob seemed to know how to touch her the way she liked.

As they kissed, he slid his hands up and down her thigh, causing her flesh to grow goosebumps. Both of them were so turned on. Rob pulled Shanta's crop top off over her head and then removed her bra, exposing her pretty titties. She returned the favor and pulled his sweatshirt off over his head, and admired his tatted-up chest. A soft moan escaped her lips once Rob licked his tongue over her erect nipple. He then orally messaged each of her breasts while Shan allowed her head to fall back and enjoyed the feeling. Standing up from the couch, Rob and Shan stepped outta their bottoms. She pushed him back down onto the couch and then straddled his lap, slowly lowering her wet, tight pussy onto his long, stiff dick.

"Mmm, yes, Rob. It feels so damn good, baby!" Shanta moaned as she bounced on Rob's lap allowing his hardness to dig deep inside of her. She liked how he sucked on her erect nipples and palmed her ass in both hands.

"Do that, boo, ride this dick," Rob groaned. He lifted her up to the tip of his dick and then slammed her down to its base repeatedly, and she tossed back her head, enjoying the pleasure. Standing up from the couch with Shanta's legs wrapped around his waist, Rob drilled deep inside her wetness. She raked her manicure over his back and moaned his name aloud. Feeling a nut swell up in the tip of his dick, Rob laid Shan back on the couch and then knelt in between her legs. He began flicking his tongue over her clit.

Shanta palmed the back of Rob's head and purred, "You better not stop eating this pussy." Her back arched off the couch as she pressed his mouth down onto her crotch, and Rob slipped two fingers in and out of her pussy while he orally pleased her. She loved the warmness of Rob's tongue and the softness of his lips on her. He sucked and licked her twat until her body racked with orgasm. "Oooh, yesss! I'm cumming!"

"Damn boo, you taste so good," Rob told her. After tasting Shan's juices, he turned her around and slipped his dick inside of her snug pussy walls from behind. "You like that shit? Tell me how much you like it."

"Yaaas, I like it so fuckin' much, baby!"

"Shit girl, you got a nigga ready to bust a nut!" Rob felt a nut swell up in the tip of his dick. As he thrust deep in Shan, she threw it back, taking the dick. Rob held her at the waist and beat the pussy up. After several thrusts, he pulled out and squirted warm semen on her ass cheeks. Exhausted, Rob sat on the couch out of breath, and Shanta sat on his lap and kissed his neck. "Shan, I really do love your lil ass."

"And... I love... you too," Shan responded in between kisses. She drew back and looked him in the eyes. "Rob, I only want to focus on being with you, so just forget whatever you wanted to talk to me about pertaining to Don." The look in her eyes told Rob that she was still hurt over Don and just didn't want to feel that way anymore.

"A'ight Shan. But whenever you wanna talk about it, then I'm here for you." Rob figured that it was best he told her the truth eventually.

CHAPTER 16

"So, last night I hit Danger for like two Gs in a dice game, right, and he wanted to keep gamblin'," T-Mac was saying. He rode shotgun while Rich pushed the Lexus. "Then, after I broke his ass, he asked if I'll give him half the money back. Can you believe that nigga?" He chuckled.

Rich pulled to a stoplight on 35th and Center Street. "Danger knows he wouldn't give half of shit back had he won the money. That nigga trippin'," he responded.

"Same shit I was thinkin'."

"Enough about that. We still need to figure out who the hell this nigga Rob is."

T-Mac puffed the blunt of za. "With money on his head, I'm sure somethin' bound to shake with the bitch-ass nigga soon. I'm just hopin' I be the one to burn his ass instead of anyone else."

"Let's just hope the nigga is still in town."

"Straight up."

They were on their way to Angie's place. It had been a couple of weeks since Rich had any time to go and check in on her. And little did he know, she had relapsed and was hiding it from him. Pulling up to Angie's home, Rich parked out front near the curb. He knew Angie was there because her car was parked in the driveway. Rich and T-Mac stepped out the whip and then made their way inside. Rich noticed most of the lights were off as he and T-Mac made their way through the house, and he wondered what it was about since it was only afternoon. T-Mac found his way into the kitchen directly for the fridge, while Rich headed for his mom's bedroom. Upon entering the room, Rich found Angie lying in bed in the dark.

"Ma, I came by to check on you. Are you okay?" Rich wanted to know.

"Y-yes, I'm okay Rich," Angie deceived. She didn't want him to see her all beat up because she knew he'd have tons of questions. After being beat by Swindle, that was a wake-up call for Angie. She hadn't done drugs since and swore to never do any again.

"What are you doin' with all of the lights out?" Rich switched on the bedroom light and saw that his mom's face was bruised and swollen. He hurried over to her and said, "What the hell happened to you?!"

"It was nothing." Her voice was close to a whisper.

"Ma, it doesn't look like nothin'. What ain't you tellin' me because whoever did this can't get away with it."

Angie could see the anger in his eyes. It was hard for her to have to tell him everything, but she knew she had to. "Rich... I don't want you to be disappointed in me, but I went back to doing drugs only to cope with the loss of your brother. I know it was the wrong way to go about it, but I didn't know what else to do. Just know that I swear to never do drugs again." Tears wet her cheeks.

"Ma, I can understand why you went back to drugs. I just wish that you woulda come to me instead so I could try and help you through this hard time. Losin' Don has been hard on me as well, so we need each other to get through this. I know that I haven't been there for you much in the past, but I'm here for you now," he expressed.

"It makes me feel better knowing that."

"Good. Now, I need to know, who did this to you?"

Angie hung her head. "It was Swindle."

"Swindle! Don had already warned his ass to stay away from you, and now this," Rich said, his tone filled with anger.

T-Mac entered the room eating a sandwich. Immediately, he noticed his auntie was all beat up. "I'ont know what happened, but whoever did this to you is as good as dead!" he raved, losing his appetite.

"It was that nigga Swindle. He has another thing comin' if thinks that he can harm anyone close to me and get away with it," Rich stated.

"There's something else you should know," Angie spoke up. "After beating me, Swindle mentioned having something to do with what happened to Don."

Rich and T-Mac looked to one another. If they needed any more reason to go after Swindle, this was more than enough.

"Trust me, Ma, Swindle won't get away with what he did to you and Don," Rich solemnly swore.

"Richard," Angie called behind him as he turned for the door, stopping him in his tracks. "I can't stand to lose both of my sons, so it's better him than you."

Without any further words, Rich proceeded on his way out with T-Mac in tow. He understood what his mom meant, and Rich had it in mind to make sure that he was there for his mom after all.

•••

Later that night, Rich, T-Mac, and Danger pulled up in a low-key sedan and parked down the street from Swindle's trap house. Rich was strapped with a Glock .40 holding an extended clip, T-Mac a Tec-9, and Danger a Mossberg pump. After what Swindle had done to Angie and what she told Rich about him mentioning having something to do with Don's murder, Rich, T-Mac, and Danger wanted to leave Swindle dead. But there were still some unanswered questions, although more than likely, they would shoot first and ask questions later.

"Think Swindle was the one who set up Don?" T-Mac asked as he checked his weapon.

"I think it's no coincidence that the nigga Rob just so happened to murk Don and then sold the bricks to Swindle n'em," Rich answered. He figured there was more to the puzzle, and Swindle had to be the centerpiece.

"Then we gotta make Swindle talk. Maybe he can tell us where to find that nigga Rob."

"Or we smoke his ass instead of talk," Danger pressed.

"A'ight. Let's run up in this trap and hit Swindle's ass up," T-Mac told him.

Rich cocked back the slide of his weapon. "Let's hit his ass up then."

Before stepping out of the sedan, Rich pulled his hood over his head, T-Mac pulled his snapback cap down low over his eyes, and Danger was barefaced. They hurried through the night towards the trap spot with guns in hand. They came upon one of Swindle's niggas that was posted on the front porch, who went for the pistol on his waist.

Boom, boom!

T-Mac popped the nigga twice in the chest, which caused him to crumple onto the porch steps. As they proceeded towards the front door, Rich dumped one more bullet in the nigga's dome before stepping over the dead body. With no hesitation, Danger kicked in the door, and the trio bombarded inside the trap. One nigga emerged from the kitchen bustin' at them, and Rich, T-Mac, and Danger busted back, filling him with bullets. They noticed Swindle running for the backdoor while another two of his niggas covered him. As the trio went for the backdoor, Swindle's niggas aired them out, which caused them to duck out the way of flying bullets. Not wanting to allow Swindle to get away, Rich left T-Mac and Danger to deal with Swindle's shooters while he hurried out the back door after Swindle.

Blocka, Blocka!

Boc, boc, boc, boc!

As soon as Rich emerged from the backdoor, Swindle shot at him over his shoulder, and Rich exchanged shots. With each pull of their triggers, their shots exploded in the quiet night and lit up the darkness, and bullets whizzed by them both. During the rapid gunshots, Rich was hit by one of Swindle's shots in the right thigh, which caused Rich to collapse onto the ground.

"Argh, shit!" Rich cried out and grabbed at his wounded leg.

Swindle seized the opportunity to walk up with his gun trained on Rich's chest and growled, "Lemme guess, you came gunnin' for me behind the shit I did to Angie."

"Nigga, you also had somethin' to do with Don bein' murked. I shoulda known!"

"Don got in the way, so I had his ass removed. And now I'ma do the same to you. Your crackhead-ass mommy can visit both her bitch-ass sons' graves!"

Rich wanted to kill Swindle more than anything, but he was in no position to do so, even though his pole was in arms reach. "Do what you gotta do," he hissed.

"Done," Swindle assured and then squeezed the trigger...

Boom, boom, boom, boom, boom!

Before Swindle was able to pull the trigger on Rich, Danger came hurrying out the backdoor after smokin' the shooters inside the trap house. He then sent shots at Swindle. Immediately turning for his Chrysler that was parked behind the trap house, Swindle began to jump inside the whip when Danger had shot him in the shoulder blade. Even with the pain Swindle was in, he jumped in the whip and peeled off down the alleyway while Danger decorated the Chrysler with bullet holes until it turned out of sight.

T-Mac emerged from the house and hurried over to his cousin's side. "You a'ight, Rich?"

"Yeah. Nigga only shot me in the leg. It's just a flesh wound," Rich replied as T-Mac helped him up onto his feet. "Woulda been over for my ass if you and Danger didn't have my back."

"Then good thing we got your back. I just hate that nigga Swindle got away," Danger said, frustrated.

"Don't trip. We'll get that pussy-ass nigga," T-Mac assured.

"Now let's get the fuck outta here before twelve shows up," Rich told them.

Once they hurried inside the sedan, T-Mac sped away from the scene while Rich sat in the passenger seat and Danger the back. It bothered Rich that Swindle had fucked around and gotten away, although he was grateful that T-Mac and Danger had been there to spare him from Swindle's bullets. He knew that Swindle would retaliate, so they had to be on point in the streets.

•••

Weed smoke clouded the interior of Swindle's Chrysler as he pushed the whip while Vito rode shotgun, who Swindle had picked up in order to have some security. They were on their way to the hospital. Since Rich had come after him, Swindle knew it was best that he lay low until he figured out how to get rid of his problem. The only person who he trusted around him at the moment was Vito, mainly because he knew that Vito had it out for Rich, and Swindle planned to use that to his advantage.

It was late night out, so motorists had their car headlights on. Traffic was light as Swindle zipped through the streets. "Can't believe Rich had the balls to come after me like that! I'ont know about you, but I want that nigga dead. And he would be if it wasn't for Danger sparin' his ass," Swindle raved. He was hurting from the bullet he had taken in the shoulder.

"I feel you, dawg. Rich ass pulled up on me in traffic lettin' off, and he smoked Q. I can't let that shit go," Vito responded.

Swindle braked at a stoplight. "Q was a real nigga. And you already know if it was the other way around, then he would ride out for you."

"Facts," Vito agreed. He took a pull of the blunt. "I'ma ride or die for Q, so when the time is right, then that bitch-ass nigga Rich gonna feel my heat."

"This time, make sure you smoke Rich and whoever is with him. We don't need them niggas out for some get back." Swindle needed for Vito to take out Rich, so he could get back to chasin' a bag. He understood that the enemy of his enemy was his best ally.

Once the light flipped green, Swindle pulled off in traffic with money on his mind. Vito rode along with his mind on murder.

Martell "Troublesome" Bolden

CHAPTER 17

Parker entered the hair salon where Shanta and Kat were already there awaiting their hairstylists for the hair appointments they had routinely scheduled. This was the first they were seeing her in nearly two weeks. As of lately, the trio of friends hardly seen one another, mainly due to Parker's absence because she was spending most of her time with Castle. And after meeting Castle during the dinner party and learning that he was a drug boss, which Parker was trafficking drugs for, it bothered Shan and Kat so much so that the two had discussed the issue and agreed that it was best that they talk to their girl about their concerns. The way they saw things is, it is one thing to be with a drug boss. It is another thing to be part of his drug ring.

Trina noticed Parker enter. "Hey, girl! Parker, I'll be with you as soon as I finish up with my client," she said, having Parker penciled in for an appointment. Trina had established Parker as a regular in order to juice her for as much information as she could get on Castle. And Parker was apparently oblivious to Trina's tactic being that Parker never ceased to give up info through her gossiping, which Trina reported to Rob.

"Okay, Trina," Parker responded. She offered her girls a hug before taking a seat beside them. "So, how have you two been doing?"

"Wouldn't you know, bitch, if your ass was around more," Kat shaded her.

"What Kat is trying to say is you haven't been around as much lately," Shan chimed in.

Parker didn't realize her girls were feeling neglected. "Look, it's nothing against you at all. I've just been focusing on my relationship with Castle."

"Listen, Parker," Shanta shifted towards her. "Are you sure that you and Castle have a healthy relationship?"

"Because we don't want him just using you," Kat added.

Parker couldn't believe her girls were coming for her. "How could you two even think like that about Castle?"

"He has no business having you doing whatever you're doing for him," Shanta said.

"Shan, it's none of you or Kat's business what I do for Castle. And for the record, the only thing I choose to do for him is drive to pick up loads and bring them to him. It's not like I'm doing anything wrong," she said in defense.

Kat placed a hand on Parker's knee and replied, "Girl, what's wrong is you putting yourself on the line for his ass."

"Well, he takes good care of me, as long as I do what I have to for him. The new Benz, the expensive bags, and the coins in my pocket aren't free."

"Is any of it worth putting yourself on the line? You're worth more than cars and bags," Shan told her.

"I thought you two were happy for me, but I guess I thought wrong!" Parker griped and jumped to her feet.

"Parker, we are—"

"I don't want to hear anymore," Parker intervened, cutting off Shanta. "If you two don't like me being with Castle, then maybe I don't need to be friends with y'all!"

Shanta stood. "Really, Parker?"

"Really," Parker replied. She grabbed up her handbag. "Trina, I'll reschedule my appointment with you because right now, I'd rather not be around these bitches." With no further words, she headed out.

Kat halted Shanta from going after Parker. "Let her ass go, Shan. She needs some time to realize we're her friends and only want what's best for her."

It bothered Shanta that things grew heated with Parker because she always wanted things to be cool with her and her friends. Although she had to admit that Kat was right, Parker needed to realize that they were only looking out for her best interest.

Overhearing the girls mention Castle had caught Trina's ear. She eavesdropped in the hopes of gathering more information, and now she had more to take back to Rob.

•••

"Fuck this nigga at?"

Rob's patience was running thin while he, TJ, and Max awaited Bone. They were seated in a booth inside the poolhall. Rob had called the gang there to further discuss the lick on Castle. He wanted to be sure they were on the same page, particularly Bone, because he noticed that as of lately, Bone seemed off.

"I told Bone's ass to be here a half-hour ago," Rob griped.

TJ took a swig from his glass of Cognac. "Well, if he isn't here soon, then I'm out. Ain't gonna keep lettin' Bone do whatever-the-fuck he wants." His tone was bitter.

"Bone will be here, a'ight," Max remarked.

Rob peeped at two niggas seated at the bar exchanging whispered words between them. Suddenly, they got up and made their way for the exit. Maybe he was just being 'noid knowing that the bounty was still on his head. However, it made him rest easy, having the FN on his waist. As he observed the two suspect niggas exit the poolhall, Bone just so happened to be entering and bypassing them. Rob shook his fuckin' head and mused, *This nigga knows I'ont like whenever he's fuckin' late.*

Before making his way over to the gang, Bone stopped at the bar and ordered himself a bottle of Budweiser. He then slid into the booth beside Max and said, "Hell is this about?"

"It's about the lick on Castle. I wanted to make sure we all know what's the move when we lay the nigga down," Rob told him.

"What else, we murk 'em all and keep movin'," Bone stated.

"This lick won't be as simple as the others. Castle keeps shooters on deck, so we're gonna have to move with finesse if we wanna make it out alive."

"Fuck all that. The only thing I need to know is when do we move on his ass," Bone remarked.

"In a few days, we'll have a window of opportunity."

"All that matters to me is the lick."

"It's not all about you, Bone," TJ piped in, his tone disapproving. "We're all in this together."

Bone scoffed and then took a swig of his beer. "TJ, let's not forget that you're the one whose plan is to walk out on us. So, miss me with that shit."

"Y'all niggas need to chill with that shit," Max spoke up.

TJ sat his glass on the table with a thud. "Fuck you sayin' Bone, huh?"

"All I'm sayin' is don't wait until after the lick, since you gonna walk out on us any-fuckin'-way, then do it now."

"Say no more. I'll give you what you want." TJ slid out of the booth and then turned for the exit.

"Yo TJ, hol' up." Max started after him until Rob put a stop to it.

"I'll go and holla at TJ," Rob told him. He narrowly eyed Bone. "You kill me with your bullshit." Rob slid out of the booth and went after TJ.

Nigga, it's either kill or be killed, Bone thought brashly as he took a sip of his beer.

"You didn't have to be like that with TJ, Bone. He's been our nigga for too damn long," Max told him.

Bone snorted. "Max, I'ont need that nigga. Been told you what I'm on, and if you ain't with it, then that's on you. I'ont know about you, but I ain't gonna let Rob or no nigga get over on me."

"Rob has never tried to get over on us. Maybe you're just gettin' greedy."

"Yeah, well, maybe. But I would rather be greedy than hungry."

Max didn't know what the hell had gotten into Bone, but he was definitely on some other shit. "Look, let's just go and check on Rob and TJ."

"Yeah, whatever."

Outside of the poolhall it was nearly night out. The sky was filled with rain clouds. Rob caught up with TJ out front. He couldn't just let TJ walk away before the lick on account of Bone. They were in this together as a gang.

"TJ, don't let the shit Bone said back there get to you," Rob told him.

"Like it or not, he's right. What the hell am I goin' on the lick for when I'm only gonna walk out on y'all afterwards," TJ replied frustratedly.

"You're goin' 'cause we can use your gun on this lick. Don't get me wrong, I trust Bone and Max, but I'd feel easier havin' you with us. I respect that you want out of the stick-up game, and so do I. I'm only askin' that you put your gun to work this one last time. Are you still down?"

TJ looked off down the street. "A'ight, I'm still down. But only this one last time."

"Then it's settled. And don't worry about Bone, I got him handled," Rob said, sure of himself.

Max and Bone came out of the poolhall and met up with the others.

"Is everything good?" Max wanted to know.

"Yeah. It's good," Rob answered. He looked to Bone. "Look, TJ's goin' with us on this lick, so you need to just accept that. We're all gonna need to watch each other's backs."

"Yeah, a'ight," Bone replied, seething.

Rob just wanted the gang to be ready to mask up and rob and kill. He knew that the lick on Castle would be deadly. Therefore, he had every intention of making it out with the goods alive.

•••

Rob and Shanta were at the lakefront drinking in the beautiful sun that dipped into the body of water off in the distance, and the sky was pinkish. Standing near the bay while waves came up under their feet, Rob held Shanta at her small waist from behind as they watched the sunset. She felt good in his arms like she belonged there. He enjoyed the feel of her frame against his, not wanting to ever let her go. Their thoughts drifted into the air.

"Isn't this sunset beautiful? I can look at it forever," Shanta said.

"Now you know exactly how I feel about you," Rob replied and then pecked her on the cheek.

"Aww, you're so sweet! It's like whenever I'm with you, things just feel right."

"I know what you mean. Whenever I'm not with you, then I can't get you off my mind."

"Well, you better not have your mind in the gutter," she half-joked.

"You know, I really do love you a lot, Shanta," he said into her ear in close to a whisper.

"And I love you too. But Rob, I just don't know if I'm ready for a serious relationship again," Shan responded in a lowered voice. She turned and looked into his eyes. "Don meant a lot to me. I just want to be with someone who'll mean something to me just as much."

Rob used his fingers to comb her hair behind her ear in order to get a better look at her facial features. "Then I can only hope that what we have can be just as meaningful," he told her genuinely.

"Hopefully."

"Look, it's gettin' late. How 'bout I get you home?" he said.

During the ride, Rob couldn't help but think about what Shanta had said back at the lakefront. Part of him found it hard to keep it a secret that he had something to do with Don being killed. To know that Don had meant so much to her ate at his conscience, mainly because he hated being part of the reason she was in pain. However, Rob was there for Shan to help ease the pain she felt.

Arriving at Shanta's place, Rob parked his Hellcat curbside. He walked her to the front door, where they embraced and shared a kiss. It was obvious the couple felt strongly for each other.

Meantime, Rich and T-Mac had just pulled up in T-Mac's Porsche SUV and parked behind Rob's Hellcat. They immediately noticed that this was the whip that belonged to Rob, and they had been in search of it for months. However, they didn't expect to see Shanta riding with Rob. The two were witnessing Shanta and Rob all over each other, who were oblivious to the eyes on them. Rich couldn't believe this shit, and T-Mac was ready to air shit out.

"Yo Rich, you seein' this shit," T-Mac said heatedly.

"I damn sure didn't see this shit comin'," Rich replied, stunned.

Rich halted his cousin as he was finna hop out of the car with a gun in hand. "Hol' up."

"Fuck you mean hol' up when the nigga who murked Don is right there," T-Mac retorted, clutching his pole.

"I just don't want you to hit up Shanta before I can get any answers outta her ass, a'ight?" He peered at T-Mac with hard eyes. After the couple's parting words, Shanta turned and entered her place. Rob hopped into his Hellcat and stabbed off down the street.

"So, what, we just gon' let the bitch-ass nigga get away," T-Mac cried out.

"Hell no. You go and take his ass out while I go and have a talk with Shan," Rich told him. Before he could completely step outta the SUV, T-Mac peeled off down the street after Rob.

Rich headed for Shanta's place with a purpose. He wanted answers, and if she couldn't give him any reasonable ones, then she would have to answer to his gun. Rich pounded on the front door, and a moment later, Shanta pulled it open and was surprised to find him there.

"Rich, what are you doing here?" Shan asked out of curiosity. Without a word, Rich stepped by her into the apartment, and she just shut the door behind him. "Mind answering my question."

"The real question is, what the hell was that nigga Rob doin' here?!" Rich pressed.

Shanta looked puzzled. "Apparently, you know Rob."

"And apparently, you don't know him as well as you think you do."

"What are you talking about, Rich?" Puzzled.

"Shan, he had a part in what happened to Don," he told her.

Hearing what Rich had said seemed to knock the breath out of Shanta. "I-I can't believe it," she stammered.

"Well, you should believe it because it's true. But maybe you know the truth already," Rich accused.

Shan eyed him sharply. "How could you think that of me?"

"How could I not when you're fuckin' with the nigga who murked my bro. Maybe it was you that set up Don."

"You know me better than that, Rich. I would never do something like that to Don. And if I would've had any idea that Rob could be the one who killed Don, then I would've never given him a chance." Tears began sliding down her cheeks.

Rich shook his damn head and said, "The only way I'll believe your tears is if you set up Rob for me."

"It's one thing to question me, and it's another to accuse me."

"Shanta, just stay away from Rob if you don't wanna put yourself in harm's way," he forewarned.

"I won't listen to no more of you coming for me, Rich. I want you out of my house now!" Shanta shoved him out of the front door and then slammed the door shut. She slid back down against the door and buried her face in her palms as she wept. She didn't know how to feel or what to think. Her mind raced, and her heart ached. Shan had never imagined that the one who'd taken Don away from her could be none other than Rob.

Meanwhile, Rob drove on his way with a lot on his mind. So much so that he wasn't mindful of T-Mac tailing him through traffic, although Rob did have his FN laying across his lap. It being later in the evening, the traffic was beginning to pick up, making it easy for T-Mac to blend in with other motorists. Now T-Mac was looking to catch Rob slippin' at the right moment.

Pulling up to a stoplight on 27th and National Street, Rob braked the whip. While awaiting the light to flip green, he thought about how there was something different about Shanta that made him want her. She was different from every other girl he had been with, but it was killing him to keep what he had done to Don from her. *Maybe it's best that I tell her the truth*, he mused. He was thinking that over, starting to pull off with traffic once the light flipped green when a car suddenly cut him off with the driver extending his arm out the window gripping a Tec-9.

Prraat, prraat, prraat!

Rob had shoved open the car door and rolled out onto the pavement just as the automatic weapon opened up into his Hellcat, shredding the frame, shattering the windows with so many bullets so fast the car seemed to lift and sway on the ground. He rolled behind the rear tire out of the way of bullets and gripped his FN.

Raising his FN over the trunk of the Hellcat, Rob fired at the vehicle attempting to kill the driver, who kept him pinned down with rapid gunfire. Rob wasn't able to get a clean shot off, so he just continued to squeeze the trigger.

T-Mac heard bullets violently striking the side of his whip and blow out its rear passenger window as Rob returned fire. Determined to leave, Rob stretched out in the street, T-Mac emptied the clip. By chance, Rob managed to duck every bullet.

The tires screeched as T-Mac stabbed off down the street. He kept his head low as he sped away while Rob filled the car with bullet holes. T-Mac was heated as hell that Rob managed to survive the brazen ambush, but he vowed to himself that he would smoke Rob's bitch-ass next time around. Rob didn't know who the hell the shooter was, although he was almost sure that it was a nigga that was out to take his head off in order to collect the bounty for the murder of Don.

As Rob fled the scene in his now bullet-riddled Hellcat, he perpetually checked his mirrors for any more tails. Taking no chances, he tightly gripped the FN in his lap while steering towards his ducked-off crib that was located approximately ten minutes outside of Milwaukee, which is where he would lay low for a day or two. Rob knew that from now on, he had to be vigilant in the streets, or he could be the next in the grave.

T-Mac returned to scoop up Rich, who was posted outside of the complex. Once he pulled to a halt in the middle of the street, Rich couldn't help but take notice of the numerous bullet holes the car had suffered, and immediately Rich hoped that T-Mac was alright and Rob was dead.

"You a'ight?" Rich asked out of concern as he stepped into the passenger seat.

T-Mac pulled off. "Yeah, I'm a'ight. But that bitch-ass nigga Rob got away."

"Not for long. We'll get that nigga sooner or later."

"What about Shanta? Why is the bitch even fuckin' with Rob when he's the one who murked Don?"

Rich snorted. "Claims that she never had an idea that Rob is responsible."

"You believe her?"

"I'ont know what to believe, but she best be tellin' the truth. If I find out that it was her idea to set up Don, then on bro's grave, I'ma put a bullet in her fuckin' head," Rich swore. He didn't want to believe that Shan had anything to do with what happened to Don, but he wouldn't throw a bullet past anyone.

CHAPTER 18

Off in the distance, lightning struck across the night sky as spatters of rain began to fall onto the windshield of Shanta's car. She pulled to the curb in front of Rob's loft complex and then cut off the engine. Shan rested her head back against the headrest and let out a sigh. What Rich had told her a few days ago about Rob being part of the reason Don was dead had Shanta's head and heart at war. Her head wanted to believe Rich, but her heart couldn't believe that Rob would do such a thing. So, she just had to find out the truth, but she was nervous about confronting him because she didn't know the outcome.

Shan stepped outta the car, making her way to the complex, and then rang the buzzer to Rob's place. A moment later, she was buzzed inside and went up to his loft. As soon as Rob opened the door while nude, without words, he pulled her into his arms and planted a trail of kisses from her lips to her neck. Shan just couldn't seem to resist the feel of him all over her.

"Rob, we need to talk," Shanta said in a whisper.

"We can talk later. Right now, I just wanna take you down," Rob replied and then kissed her passionately.

Rob lifted Shan up by her ass, and she wrapped her legs around his waist as he carried her into the bedroom, where he laid her back on the king-sized bed. There were chocolate-covered strawberries and champagne set out on the nightstand, along with lit candles positioned all around the room and slow jams playing in the background, making for a romantic setting. Rob had a night of romance planned for them, and Shanta appreciated the gesture.

Rob began stripping Shan outta her clothes until she was nude. He then dove his head in between her legs and started eating her pussy. Shanta enjoyed the feel of his lips and tongue pleasing her. His tongue rapidly stroked her clit, and she grasped the back of his skull. Her eyes were closed, and her toes curled as her back arched off the bed from the feeling of elation.

"Oooh... yeesss, Rob!" Shan groaned. Her juices covered his face. She pulled Rob's lips to hers, then tasted her own juices and guided his hardness inside her wet-shot.

"Damn baby, you so wet," Rob crooned. He found himself making love to her, and he enjoyed seeing her love faces. Shan dug her manicured nails into his back as Rob thrust deep within her, hitting her spot. "You like that?"

"Yesss, I do."

Rob tossed her legs over his shoulders and commenced beating the pussy up. Her snug slit gripped at his hardness, bringing him close to climax. He then turned Shanta around and dug in her from behind. She gripped the sheets while she threw the pussy back at him. Rob spanked her ass, and she liked it. Once again, Shan came, her juices slid down Rob's inner thighs. After filling her with his dick, Rob also reached climax.

Rob rolled beside Shanta in bed, both covered in perspiration and breathing heavily. She rested her head on his chest, and he combed his fingers through her hair. Rob couldn't deny that he loved Shanta, maybe even more than she knew. He didn't want to ever hurt her, but he knew that it would hurt her more than anything to know that he had a part in murkin' Don. Part of him really did feel the need to tell her with the hopes that she would forgive him. And Shan had to admit that she fell in love with Rob, even after she thought she'd never love anyone else after losing Don. Part of her was afraid that Rob may have played a part in what happened to Don, but she just couldn't believe it. They felt perfect for each other, but a perfect world didn't exist.

"How about we have some champagne," Rob said. He reached over and grabbed the bottle of champagne outta the bucket of ice and poured them each a glass. Lifting his glass, he toasted, "To us."

Shanta took a sip from her glass. "You know, it's nice being here with you."

"I wouldn't want to be here with anyone else." He grabbed a chocolate-covered strawberry and fed her a bite.

"What made you decide to plan such a romantic night?" She set her glass on the nightstand at her bedside.

"Wanted to show you what life would be like with me."

Spending the rest of her life with anyone besides Don was nothing Shanta never even imagined. And now, she felt lucky to have Rob in her life, yet the thought of Rob taking Don outta her life bothered her. If this was true, then Shan didn't know how her heart would take the feeling of the man she once loved more than anything being killed by the man that she now loves more than expected. Either the truth will hurt her, or it will set her free.

Shanta peered into Rob's eyes and asked, "Will you always tell me the truth, no matter how much you believe it may hurt me?"

"Of course, boo. Just know that no matter what the truth may be, it'll never be my intention to hurt you," Rob answered.

"Then there should be nothing that you keep from me."

Rob looked perplexed. "Shanta, what is this about?"

"It's about Don... I-I was told by someone close to me that you had something to do with him being robbed and killed." Shanta's voice was shaky from nerves getting the best of her.

"Shan, I know how much you loved Don, and I know losin' him the way you did hurts." He was in a dilemma, and unbeknownst to him, Rich was the one close to Shanta.

"Tell me it isn't true that you had anything to do with what happened to him, Rob." Tears rimmed her eyes.

At that moment, Rob didn't know what to tell Shanta. On the one hand, he felt the need to tell her the truth, and on the other, he felt that what she didn't know wouldn't hurt her. Whenever he was with her, his heart fluttered while at the same time he had a guilty conscience. He loved knowing that he now made her happy but hated knowing that he took her previous happiness. Now Rob had to decide whether or not he would tell her the truth.

Rob sat up on the edge of the bed with his back to Shanta, no longer able to look her in the eyes. "Listen, I... I wanna be truthful with you, Shan, and hope that you can find it in your heart to forgive me. I'm sorry to tell you that it's true. I had somethin' to do with what happened to Don. But—"

Shanta rushed onto her feet. "But nothing, Rob! I can't believe you, of all niggas, killed Don!"

"Believe me. I wanted to tell you right after I figured out you were there that night. It was just hard for me to do because I didn't wanna break your heart."

"Rob, you broke my heart when you took Don from me!" she cried.

"Shanta, I never meant for things to turn out this way between us," Rob assured. He stood to his feet and began approaching her. "Believe me or not, I love you."

"Stay the hell away from me!" Shan shouted angrily as she hurriedly pulled on her clothes.

"Even if you do love me, you'll never love me more than Don!"

After dressing herself, Shanta rushed out of the loft. Rob quickly pulled on some basketball shorts and then went after her. By the time he had caught up with her, she was already outside, jumping into her car during the thunderstorm.

Running through the downpour of rain, Rob attempted to stop Shanta, but she started the car and then skirted off down the street. He knew that she was heartbroken, and there may be nothing he could ever do to fix it.

•••

With Brittany snuggled into Rich's arms, they sat on the couch in the front room of his place, watching a Milwaukee Bucks game. In fact, Britt was at Rich's crib so much as of late that it was as if she had moved in with him. She even kept some of her lady products there, and Rich didn't mind because he enjoyed her company. It was safe to say that their relationship was serious.

While Rich was watching the ball game, Brittany kept asking him a lot of questions about the game of basketball. Instead of being annoyed by all of the questions, Rich appreciated that Britt cared enough to show interest in something that he liked. More than anything, the couple didn't mind spending time together no matter what they were doing.

Rich's iPhone rang, and he reached over, grabbing it off the end table. Checking its display, he saw the FaceTime caller was Shanta and wondered why she was calling, being that she hadn't bothered to since their last encounter. He answered, "S'up, Shan. I haven't heard from you since..."

"I know since you tried telling me that Rob had something to do with what happened to Don," Shanta intercepted. She sighed. "Well, you told me right."

"So now, all of a sudden, you believe what I told you?"

"Listen, Rich. It's not that I didn't believe you. It was just hard to believe what I was hearing about Rob. So, I decided to confront him about what you told me."

"And?"

"He confessed," she told him.

Rich quickly sat up. "You mean to tell me that he actually confessed to havin' somethin' to do with what happened to Don?"

"Yes... he did." Shanta hung her head, but not before Rich could see tears slide down her cheeks.

"Shanta, it's fucked up you had to find out that way. But at least now you know the truth."

"Rich, I just don't want you to hate me behind this situation. If I would've known that Rob had anything to do with what happened to Don, then I swear that I would've never given him a chance at all. I was so stupid not to know, and even more stupid for catching feelings for him," she expressed through tears.

"Listen, I don't hate you because I knew that you would never do anything on purpose to hurt Don. It's Rob that I have hate in my heart for behind this shit," Rich confirmed. "Shanta, just make sure you stay away from Rob because I have every killa in the city tryin' to look for his ass."

After ending the call, Rich buried his face inside the palms of his hands. *I can't believe that Rob had the heart to confess to killin' Don,* he thought, seething. *Well, I'ma make sure to rip his fuckin' heart out.* Now Rich was certain that Rob was the nigga he was after, and he wanted to get revenge by any means necessary.

"Baby, are you alright?" Brittany asked outta concern after overhearing the discussion, and she rubbed his back in comfort.

"Yeah, I'm a'ight. It's just hard knowin' that the nigga who had somethin' to do with killin' my bro has been with the only woman Don woulda killed or been killed for," Rich expressed.

"Imagine how Shan must feel. I'm sure a big part of her feels like she betrayed Don in a way, mainly because she gained feelings for the guy who had something to do with killing him. But it's not like she knew who Rob was from the start, so she isn't the one to blame."

"The only one I blame is that nigga Rob. And I won't be satisfied until he's not breathin'," Rich declared.

Without words, Rich stood and then stepped outta the room. Brittany figured that it was best to leave him alone while he gathered himself. She knew how much he was still grieving over the death of Don, and he knew how much his grief drove him towards vengeance.

•••

TJ slid into the opposite side of the booth that Rob preoccupied. It was the middle of the night, and they were meeting up at the poolhall. The hall was occupied by numerous patrons having drinks and shooting games of pool and enjoying the night. Rob had called TJ there so they could talk in person, and Bone nor Max was invited. This was about Shanta, who Rob had not heard from since she stormed out on him. He had tried calling and texting her numerous times, hoping they could work shit out, only to get no answer. And now Rob didn't know what to do besides turn to TJ for someone to lean on.

"Rob, what's so damn urgent that you had to get me outta the bed with my girl to meet with you at this time of night?" TJ wanted to know. "Shouldn't you be in bed with Shanta right about now?"

Rob took a gulp from his glass of Henny. "Shanta knows it was me," he told TJ reluctantly.

TJ looked at him wide-eyed. "But I thought she didn't know, Rob."

"I thought so too. I guess she must have heard it from someone because she confronted me about it."

"And what did you tell her?"

"What was I supposed to tell her, TJ?" Rob replied, sounding aggravated.

"You were supposed to tell her ass that it wasn't you!" TJ responded emphatically.

Rob hung his head and stared into his nearly empty glass of Henny, and in a lowered voice, he said, "Well, I didn't. What I told her was the truth."

"Why did you tell her the truth of all things, Rob?"

"Because whenever I'm with Shanta, it weighs heavy on my mind, and I thought that by tellin' her the truth, it would somehow bring me and her closer," he admitted.

"Apparently, you thought wrong. This is exactly why I told you to forget about that girl, to begin with, and now you'll have to murk her," TJ told him.

Finally, Rob met TJ's eyes. "In my mind, I know you're right. But in my heart, I just can't do it."

"Rob, Shanta's the one and the only person that actually knows it was you who murked Don. That could go wrong in so many different ways for not only you but the whole gang. It's not like you didn't have the heart to murk her before; she just so happened to survive. And now she can point you out if need be. You know the rule: murk 'em all and keep movin'," he expounded.

"Look, TJ. I can't just murk Shanta because I know she still loves me."

"Or perhaps, she hates you now that she knows you murked Don."

"Whether she love me or hate me, I need to try and figure shit out with Shanta. Either respect it or not, that's on you,"

Rob told him. He polished off the remains of his drink before sliding outta the booth and then exiting the poolhall.

Even though TJ didn't agree with Rob's decision, he did begrudgingly respect it, the same way in which Rob had respected him deciding to be with Kayla. And being that Rob was his ace nigga, TJ wanted to support him on his decision no matter what. He slid outta the booth and then hurried outside, where he caught up with Rob, who he halted from stepping into his Hellcat.

"Even if I don't agree with your decision, I respect it. So, I have your back," TJ assured.

"Good. Because you already know there's a lot of niggas plottin' behind my back," Rob half-joked.

"All jokes aside, you can't let Bone or Max find out about what's goin' on with Shanta. We both know that they'll want her dead ASAP, especially Bone since he's not ever tryin' to end up on lockdown again. Or worse, in a grave. Because now she has the means to be the cause of either."

Rob knew that TJ had a point. "Then before either of them finds out, I'll figure shit out with Shanta, no matter what I have to do," he declared.

"No doubt." TJ understood that Rob would do whatever was in the best interest of the gang. "Look, why don't you go home and get some sleep."

"I can sleep when I die. Instead, I'ma slide through the streets and clear my head." Rob noticed the worried expression etched on TJ's face, so Rob lifted his shirt just enough to reveal the butt of his Glock and added, "Don't worry about me, 'cause I ain't worried about nothin'."

After the two dapped up, they entered their vehicles and then parted ways. During the ride home, TJ couldn't help but think about all that was unfolding, and he hoped it wouldn't turn out bad. While cruising the streets, Rob tried to figure out what was best, and he wanted to make sure all was good. They each understood that in the game, a nigga had to be willing to take the good with the bad.

CHAPTER 19

During the ride, Rich noticed that Angie was awfully quiet. He could tell that there was something occupying her head-space. After Angie had spent two weeks in the rehabilitation center, Rich was now taking her home. Arriving at Angie's home, Rich pulled his Lexus curbside out front and parked. Angie was happy to finally be back home and no longer have to spend another night in the center. The comfort of knowing she would be safe and sound in her own home was a good feeling, although it was bittersweet being that the house reminded her of Don.

"Ma, I know it's not easy for you to talk about, but I do understand why you relapsed. Trust me, losin' Don isn't easy for me neither," Rich told her.

"I just feel like I failed you and Don once again due to my drug addiction. For once, I just want to be the mother you two deserve to have in life," Angie responded on the verge of tears.

Rich stroked her back in comfort. "Don always told me that you're the only mom we have, so no matter what, we should love you. And now I understand what he meant. Listen, Ma. I'm here for you, and I believe in you."

"And you can believe this time I'll stay clean no matter what. I just want to make you and Don proud of me."

"You already have. And I'm sure Don would agree."

"I hate that I let Swindle take advantage of my addiction. Well, I won't ever let that happen again," she assured.

"I'll make sure you won't have to ever again worry about Swindle," he declared. His mom understood what he meant.

Angie shifted towards him. "Richard," she began in a lowered voice, "you know how much it devastated me to lose Donte. I don't want to lose you too."

"Ma, if I lose my life, then I want you to know that I love you."

"And I love you too, son."

"Ma, I'ma get goin'. Just call if you need me for anything," Rich said.

"Stay safe in these streets," she told him.

Rich leaned over, then kissed her forehead, and a tear crept down Angie's cheek. It was obvious that losing Don had devastated both of them in different ways because Don had always been there to make sure they both didn't have many worries. So, Rich could understand why his mom turned to drugs in order to cope, and she understood why Rich turned to the streets in order to fill a void. And they each had the understanding that without Don, then they needed to be there for each other.

After dropping off his mom, Rich headed to the hood in order to scoop up T-Mac. He stopped at the trap, then T-Mac came out and stepped into the passenger seat. They set off to catch some plays.

"Just came from droppin' off my OG. I hope she stays clean," Rich commented as he steered around an SUV in traffic.

"So, how's Auntie Angie?" T-Mac asked.

"She's doin' better. I just wanna do what Don would want me to do for our mom. Feel me?"

"Yeah, I feel you, cuz. Plus, Don would want you to smoke Swindle for what he did to your mom."

Rich zipped the Lexus through a yellow light. "Fa sho."

"Now that we're done dealin' with the bitch-ass nigga Swindle, we gotta find a plug like ASAP," T-Mac mentioned.

"I'm already on it. In between time, we need to find Swindle and smoke his ass," Rich replied.

"Say no more."

"Listen, just know that we won't stop til we're on top in these streets."

After catching some plays, Rich and T-Mac were on their way back to the hood. Being that it was later in the evening, the skies were tinted orangish, and Rich had the headlights of his Lexus beaming as he moved the coup through traffic. While riding shotgun, T-Mac counted up the paper-cheese that was just accumulated. They both had their poles in their lap, just in case.

Needing some petrol, Rich stopped at the gas station in the hood. T-Mac decided he'd go and pay for the gas and purchase a box of blunts while he was at it, and before stepping outta the whip, he tucked his pole on his person. While Rich was posted outside near the car pumping the gas, he left his pole lying across his seat. Rich noticed T-Mac was inside the station choppin' it up with one of the hood rats. As he was finna step into the Lex' after filling the gas tank, Rich peeped the sedan with tinted windows pull into the lot, and before he knew what was coming, the passenger door flew opened then out came Vito gripping a choppa.

Boc, boc, boc, boc!

Flames spit from the barrel of the choppa as Vito walked towards the Lex' lettin' off. Rich dove beside the Lex for cover. He didn't have time to grab his pole in order to return fire. The rapid gunfire kept him pinned down, so now Rich was a sitting duck. Just on the opposite side of the car, Vito decorated it with bullet holes and shattered its windows. Once Vito made his way around the trunk of the Lex', he came upon a helpless Rich on the pavement. The two locked eyes as Vito trained the choppa down on Rich.

Blocka, blocka, blocka!

Before Vito could pull the trigger on Rich, he was struck in the arm by gunfire from T-Mac. Instantly, Vito turned his weapon and shot back at T-Mac. As Vito hurried to the sedan, he and T-Mac exchanged shots, and bullets whizzed past them both. When Vito ducked into the sedan, it then sped outta the lot with T-Mac airin' it out. Once the sedan was gone, T-Mac hurried over to Rich and helped him to his feet, and then they hurried into the shot-up Lexus.

"Can't believe that nigga, Vito, came for me," Rich said as he sped outta the lot.

"Well, believe it. And I'm sure he was sent by Swindle," T-Mac replied. "I'm sure he was the shooter that Swindle sent to shoot up our trap."

"Then we'll smoke Swindle and Vito before they can come for us again," Rich vowed.

CHAPTER 20

"There the nigga is now."

While sitting in the Lexus SUV parked down the block from the hair salon, Rob, TJ, Max, and Bone lurked on their mark, Castle. They observed as Castle pulled his ruby red Bentley to the curb before the salon, not to mention the matching Bentley truck trailing. A moment later, Parker emerged from the salon, and Rob thought the bitch looked familiar, but he couldn't put a name to the face. She entered Castle's Bentley, and then Castle pulled off into traffic with them goons behind him.

Tailing their mark, Rob rode shotgun while TJ drove, and Max and Bone took up the backseat. They were each armed with heavy artillery, knowing what they were up against. Unlike marks they'd robbed and killed before, going after Castle was a risk. However, high risk means a high reward. All Rob wanted was for him and his gang to make it out with the goods alive. But life insurance isn't part of the game.

The gang kept a distance in traffic as they tailed so not to be made. They were led to Castle's mini-mansion, where the Bentley and Bentley truck pulled onto the horseshoe driveway. The goons stepped out of the Bentley truck on security as Castle and Parker exited his Bentley. Suddenly, the Lexus sped onto the driveway behind both vehicles, and then Rob n'em hopped out wearing masks and leveling firearms.

Boc, boc, boc, boc!

Prraat, prraat, prraat!

Castle's goons opened fire on Rob n'em, causing them to duck beside the Lexus as they fired back. Bullets zipped by those on either side. The goons refused to get down, so Rob n'em would have to make them lay down. In the midst of the shootout, Castle snatched up Parker, using her as a human shield as he backed his way into the home while firing his Glock. Once making it inside, he hurriedly locked the door. Castle didn't know where the jack-boys had come from, but he was convinced it was a setup, and the only person he could think would do so was Parker.

"Bitch!" Castle barked and shoved Parker onto the floor, aiming his Glock on her. "You set me up?"

"No, Castle! I wouldn't do you like that!" Parker cried.

"Then why the fuck did them niggas tail us after pickin' your ass up? Who are they, Parker, and don't you lie to me?" he demanded. As Parker tried getting up from the floor, Castle kicked her back down.

"Castle, I swear on my life, I don't know what's going on or who they are. The only person I told anything about you is Trina at the salon. Please, trust me," she pled for her life.

"Neva trust a big butt and a smile."

Blam!

Castle shot Parker in the head, ruining her fresh hairdo with a slug, and she died almost instantly. He didn't trust her ass. Although Parker wasn't exactly at fault, she'd just never realized how much danger she put him in by running her mouth so fuckin' much about his business at the salon.

Hearing the wooden front door being forcefully kicked, Castle registered that it was the jack-boys attempting to force their way inside. Rob n'em had managed to lay down the goons and were now ready to carry out their plot to rob and kill Castle's ass. Castle turned his aim and fired shots at them through the door, causing Rob n'em to duck out of the way as bullets ripped through the timber. After a few moments, the shots subsided once Castle emptied his extended clip. It gave Rob n'em the chance to kick in the door and barge inside, each with their guns leveled on their mark.

"A'ight, a'ight!" Castle cried in surrender and tossed the gun onto the floor, then threw his hands up. "Y'all can take whatever. Just don't kill me."

"Nigga, where the stash at?" Rob demanded.

"How do I know you won't kill me if I give you what you want?"

"You don't know. Now take us to the stash!"

With no resistance, Castle led them into the den with Rob's barrel stuffed to his back. Castle went over to the closet, where he showed them the money, and dope was stashed away beneath the floorboards. TJ and Max began tossing the numerous stacks of the cash and numerous keys of coke into a duffel bag, which Bone held open. There was more cash and bricks there than they'd ever come up on at once.

"There's at least six-hundred Gs and ten birds. A'ight man, I gave y'all what y'all came for. Now let me live," Castle bargained.

Rob disregarded his attempt to bargain and stated, "Nigga, before you even knew it, you were dead." He pressed the muzzle to Castle's dome and pulled the trigger...

Rrraaa, rrraaa!

At that moment, one of Castle's goons, who managed to barely survive being riddled with bullets, came staggering into the den with his AR-15 in hand, and the goon let off. Rounds wildly sprayed throughout the den, leaving bullet holes in whatever they encountered. As the shots were fired, Rob and Bone instantaneously turned their aims on the goon and fired back, filling him with bullets and leaving him murked for sure. Although Max hadn't moved quickly enough out the path of the goon's gunfire and he had taken a shot to the left side of his torso, which knocked his ass off his feet and hurt like hell. But it was TJ who caught the worse bullet that struck him in the back of the dome, blowing out his brains.

This wasn't part of the plan. The plan was to get in and get out alive.

Rob hurried over to his dead homie and cried out, "This isn't how shit s'posed to go, TJ!"

"C'mon, Rob, we gotta get the fuck outta here!" Bone urged.

Grabbing up the duffel bag, Bone rushed outta the den, and reluctantly Rob followed as he assisted a wounded Max. Though they had collected all they had come for, they were leaving behind something most valuable, their fallen comrade, TJ. And perhaps thy may regret not murkin' Castle in vengeance.

Once the gang of jack-boys had rushed out, Castle picked himself up from the floor. He knew he was fortunate to be alive. Although now he was out of all of his fortunes. *Them niggas took every-fuckin'-thing*, Castle mused heatedly. They gonna wish they also took my life.

•••

The gang sped away from Castle's mini-mansion in the Lexus. Rob drove while Bone rode shotgun with the duffel bag containing the money and drugs on his lap, and a badly wounded Max laid across the backseat. One person that was missing was TJ after being killed. During the lick, shit went bad.

"Can't fuckin' believe TJ got smoked back there. We were s'posed to watch each other's backs," Rob fumed as he sped through traffic.

"Ain't our fuckin' fault. Nigga shoulda gotten out of the game when he still had a chance. Now it's game over," Bone remarked. He perpetually checked the mirrors for anything amiss.

Rob glanced over at him with hard eyes and raved, "TJ gave his damn life for us!"

"And that's just part of the life we live," Bone retorted unremorsefully.

Rob abruptly veered to the curb, grabbed Bone by the collar, and stated, "If it wasn't for TJ, then we'd all be dead!"

"You're the one who wanted TJ on the lick, Rob. So, he's dead because of you!" Bone retorted in anger and brushed Rob's hand away.

"Say what you want, Bone."

Bone's claim had cut Rob deep. Rob couldn't help but feel at fault for TJ's death because he was the one who had convinced TJ to come along on the lick, even when TJ didn't want to. Then again, he knew TJ was down to ride or die. Rob just didn't want him to die in the way he did.

"W-will you two niggas stop fightin' for a m-moment," Max breathed. He nursed his wounded side in an attempt to slow down the bloodstream as blood seeped through the crevices of his fingers. The AR-15 round he had taken, left him in bad shape.

"How you holdin' up back there, Max?" Rob wanted to know, looking at him through the rearview mirror.

Max winced in pain. "Don't worry, I'm good," he deceived.

"Maybe we should get you to the hospital."

"Max says he's good," Bone cut in. "There's no need for him to go to the hospital gettin' any unwanted attention. 'Cause if we take him there, then he'll be questioned by Twelve. And we don't need that shit."

"I'm just tryna do what's best for him, Bone," Rob replied sternly.

"Let's j-just get to the hotel and get off the street," Max told them.

Arriving at the Diamond Inn, Rob parked the Lex' and then helped Max into the hotel while Bone carried the duffel. Inside their room, Rob assisted Max into a chair, and Bone sat the duffel on the table. Their heads were still spinning from the lick, which didn't exactly go as planned. And now the gang was left without TJ.

Rob stepped over to the window and looked out at the city lights. "Still can't believe TJ ain't here with us."

"Now what are w-we gonna do with his cut of t-the money?" Max wanted to know.

"TJ's dead. He won't be needin' any money in the grave," Bone scoffed.

"But on behalf of TJ, we'll give his portion to Kayla," Rob told them. He noticed Bone cut sharp eyes at him. "Got a problem with that, Bone?"

Bone stepped to him and retorted, "And what if I do, Rob?"

"Then--"

"Argh, shit!" Max grimaced in pain and doubled over. He was bleeding profusely, and the pain was excruciating.

Rob hurried over to Max, holding him upright. "Max, we need to get you to the hospital before you bleed out."

"N-no... I'll live," Max assured.

"Don't be so sure of that." Bone held his gun leveled on Max's dome.

Max peered at him with disappointment in his eyes and uttered, "Why do it like this, Bone?"

"What can I say? The money made me do it." Bone squeezed the trigger with no remorse.

Boc, boc, boc!

The shots to Max's dome put him out of his misery, and the corpse slumped from the chair onto the floor at the feet of Rob and Bone. Subsequently, Bone turned his aim on Rob, and the two stared one another dead in the eyes. Unbeknownst to Rob, betraying the gang had been part of Bone's ploy the entire time. He'd take the money and dope for himself, even if it meant having to spill his comrade's blood.

"You won't be able to live with this shit on your conscience, Bone," Rob told him while staring down the barrel with no sign of fear etched on his face.

Bone scoffed and stated, "I'll do anything for the money. It's not even on my conscience." He gave Rob a smirk before pulling the trigger in his face.

Boc!

The shot caused Rob to crumple onto the floor at Bone's feet. Blood vastly pooled around Rob's head while Bone wasted no time grabbing up the duffel bag from the table. As Bone rushed out of the room, he stepped in the blood of his comrades. He hurried into the Lexus, tossing the duffel into the passenger seat. As Bone sped away from the scene, he didn't even feel bad about leaving the same niggas who had been loyal to him for dead. Bone had chosen money over loyalty.

To Be Continued...
Money in the Grave 3
Coming Soon

Lock Down Publications and Ca$h Presents assisted publishing packages.

BASIC PACKAGE $499
Editing
Cover Design
Formatting

UPGRADED PACKAGE $800
Typing
Editing
Cover Design
Formatting

ADVANCE PACKAGE $1,200
Typing
Editing
Cover Design
Formatting
Copyright registration
Proofreading
Upload book to Amazon

LDP SUPREME PACKAGE $1,500
Typing
Editing
Cover Design
Formatting
Copyright registration
Proofreading
Set up Amazon account

Upload book to Amazon
Advertise on LDP Amazon and Facebook page

***Other services available upon request. Additional charges may apply
Lock Down Publications
P.O. Box 944
Stockbridge, GA 30281-9998
Phone # 470 303-9761

Submission Guideline

Submit the first three chapters of your completed manuscript to ldpsubmissions@gmail.com, subject line: Your book's title. The manuscript must be in a .doc file and sent as an attachment. Document should be in Times New Roman, double spaced and in size 12 font. Also, provide your synopsis and full contact information. If sending multiple submissions, they must each be in a separate email.

Have a story but no way to send it electronically? You can still submit to LDP/Ca$h Presents. Send in the first three chapters, written or typed, of your completed manuscript to:

LDP: Submissions Dept
Po Box 944
Stockbridge, Ga 30281

DO NOT send original manuscript. Must be a duplicate.

Provide your synopsis and a cover letter containing your full contact information.

Thanks for considering LDP and Ca$h Presents.

<u>NEW RELEASES</u>

KINGZ OF THE GAME by PLAYA RAY
VICIOUS LOYALTY by KINGPEN
STRAIGHT BEAST MODE by DEKARI
COKE KINGS 5 by T.J. EDWARDS
MONEY GAME 2 by SMOOVE DOLLA
LOYAL TO THE SOIL by JIBRIL WIL-
LIAMS
A GANGSTA'S PAIN by J-BLUNT
MONEY IN THE GRAVE 2 by MARTELL
"TROUBLESOME" BOLDEN

STRAIGHT BEAST MODE II

De'Kari

KINGPIN KILLAZ IV

STREET KINGS III

PAID IN BLOOD III

CARTEL KILLAZ IV

DOPE GODS III

Hood Rich

SINS OF A HUSTLA II

ASAD

RICH $AVAGE II

MONEY IN THE GRAVE II

By Martell Troublesome Bolden

YAYO V

Bred In The Game 2

S. Allen

CREAM III

By Yolanda Moore

SON OF A DOPE FIEND III

HEAVEN GOT A GHETTO II

By Renta

LOYALTY AIN'T PROMISED III

By Keith Williams

I'M NOTHING WITHOUT HIS LOVE II

SINS OF A THUG II

TO THE THUG I LOVED BEFORE II

By Monet Dragun

QUIET MONEY IV

EXTENDED CLIP III

THUG LIFE IV

By **Trai'Quan**

THE STREETS MADE ME IV

By **Larry D. Wright**

IF YOU CROSS ME ONCE II

By **Anthony Fields**

THE STREETS WILL NEVER CLOSE II

By K'ajji

HARD AND RUTHLESS III

THE BILLIONAIRE BENTLEYS II

Von Diesel

KILLA KOUNTY II

By Khufu

MONEY GAME III

By Smoove Dolla

A GANGSTA'S KARMA II

By FLAME

JACK BOYZ VERSUS DOPE BOYZ

A DOPEBOY'S DREAM III

By Romell Tukes

MURDA WAS THE CASE II

Elijah R. Freeman

THE STREETS NEVER LET GO II

By Robert Baptiste

AN UNFORESEEN LOVE III

By **Meesha**

KING OF THE TRENCHES II
by **GHOST & TRANAY ADAMS**

MONEY MAFIA II

LOYAL TO THE SOIL II

By **Jibril Williams**

QUEEN OF THE ZOO II

By **Black Migo**

THE BRICK MAN II

By King Rio

VICIOUS LOYALTY II

By Kingpen

A GANGSTA'S PAIN II

By J-Blunt

Available Now

RESTRAINING ORDER **I & II**

By **CA$H & Coffee**

LOVE KNOWS NO BOUNDARIES **I II & III**

By **Coffee**

RAISED AS A GOON I, II, III & IV

BRED BY THE SLUMS I, II, III

BLAST FOR ME I & II

ROTTEN TO THE CORE I II III

A BRONX TALE I, II, III

DUFFLE BAG CARTEL I II III IV V VI

HEARTLESS GOON I II III IV V

A SAVAGE DOPEBOY I II

DRUG LORDS I II III

CUTTHROAT MAFIA I II

KING OF THE TRENCHES

By **Ghost**

LAY IT DOWN **I & II**

LAST OF A DYING BREED I II

BLOOD STAINS OF A SHOTTA I & II III

By **Jamaica**

LOYAL TO THE GAME I II III

LIFE OF SIN I, II III

By **TJ & Jelissa**

BLOODY COMMAS I & II

SKI MASK CARTEL I II & III

KING OF NEW YORK I II,III IV V

RISE TO POWER I II III

COKE KINGS I II III IV V

BORN HEARTLESS I II III IV

KING OF THE TRAP I II

By **T.J. Edwards**

IF LOVING HIM IS WRONG…I & II

LOVE ME EVEN WHEN IT HURTS I II III

Money in the Grave 2

By **Jelissa**
WHEN THE STREETS CLAP BACK I & II III
THE HEART OF A SAVAGE I II III
MONEY MAFIA
LOYAL TO THE SOIL
By **Jibril Williams**
A DISTINGUISHED THUG STOLE MY HEART I II & III
LOVE SHOULDN'T HURT I II III IV
RENEGADE BOYS I II III IV
PAID IN KARMA I II III
SAVAGE STORMS I II
AN UNFORESEEN LOVE I II
By **Meesha**
A GANGSTER'S CODE I &, II III
A GANGSTER'S SYN I II III
THE SAVAGE LIFE I II III
CHAINED TO THE STREETS I II III
BLOOD ON THE MONEY I II III
A GANGSTA'S PAIN
By **J-Blunt**
PUSH IT TO THE LIMIT
By **Bre' Hayes**
BLOOD OF A BOSS **I, II, III, IV, V**
SHADOWS OF THE GAME
TRAP BASTARD
By **Askari**
THE STREETS BLEED MURDER **I, II & III**

165

THE HEART OF A GANGSTA I II& III

By **Jerry Jackson**

CUM FOR ME I II III IV V VI VII

An **LDP Erotica Collaboration**

BRIDE OF A HUSTLA **I II & II**

THE FETTI GIRLS **I, II& III**

CORRUPTED BY A GANGSTA I, II III, IV

BLINDED BY HIS LOVE

THE PRICE YOU PAY FOR LOVE I, II ,III

DOPE GIRL MAGIC I II III

By **Destiny Skai**

WHEN A GOOD GIRL GOES BAD

By **Adrienne**

THE COST OF LOYALTY I II III

By Kweli

A GANGSTER'S REVENGE **I II III & IV**

THE BOSS MAN'S DAUGHTERS I II III IV V

A SAVAGE LOVE **I & II**

BAE BELONGS TO ME I II

A HUSTLER'S DECEIT I, II, III

WHAT BAD BITCHES DO I, II, III

SOUL OF A MONSTER I II III

KILL ZONE

A DOPE BOY'S QUEEN I II III

By **Aryanna**

A KINGPIN'S AMBITON

A KINGPIN'S AMBITION **II**

I MURDER FOR THE DOUGH
By **Ambitious**
TRUE SAVAGE I II III IV V VI VII
DOPE BOY MAGIC I, II, III
MIDNIGHT CARTEL I II III
CITY OF KINGZ I II
NIGHTMARE ON SILENT AVE
By **Chris Green**
A DOPEBOY'S PRAYER
By **Eddie "Wolf" Lee**
THE KING CARTEL **I, II & III**
By **Frank Gresham**
THESE NIGGAS AIN'T LOYAL **I, II & III**
By **Nikki Tee**
GANGSTA SHYT **I II &III**
By **CATO**
THE ULTIMATE BETRAYAL
By **Phoenix**
BOSS'N UP **I , II & III**
By **Royal Nicole**
I LOVE YOU TO DEATH
By **Destiny J**
I RIDE FOR MY HITTA
I STILL RIDE FOR MY HITTA
By **Misty Holt**
LOVE & CHASIN' PAPER
By **Qay Crockett**

167

TO DIE IN VAIN

SINS OF A HUSTLA

By **ASAD**

BROOKLYN HUSTLAZ

By **Boogsy Morina**

BROOKLYN ON LOCK I & II

By **Sonovia**

GANGSTA CITY

By **Teddy Duke**

A DRUG KING AND HIS DIAMOND I & II III

A DOPEMAN'S RICHES

HER MAN, MINE'S TOO I, II

CASH MONEY HO'S

THE WIFEY I USED TO BE I II

By Nicole Goosby

TRAPHOUSE KING **I II & III**

KINGPIN KILLAZ I II III

STREET KINGS I II

PAID IN BLOOD **I II**

CARTEL KILLAZ I II III

DOPE GODS I II

By **Hood Rich**

LIPSTICK KILLAH **I, II, III**

CRIME OF PASSION I II & III

FRIEND OR FOE I II III

By **Mimi**

STEADY MOBBN' **I, II, III**

THE STREETS STAINED MY SOUL I II

By **Marcellus Allen**

WHO SHOT YA **I, II, III**

SON OF A DOPE FIEND I II

HEAVEN GOT A GHETTO

Renta

GORILLAZ IN THE BAY **I II III IV**

TEARS OF A GANGSTA I II

3X KRAZY I II

STRAIGHT BEAST MODE

DE'KARI

TRIGGADALE I II III

MURDAROBER WAS THE CASE

Elijah R. Freeman

GOD BLESS THE TRAPPERS I, II, III

THESE SCANDALOUS STREETS I, II, III

FEAR MY GANGSTA I, II, III IV, V

THESE STREETS DON'T LOVE NOBODY I, II

BURY ME A G I, II, III, IV, V

A GANGSTA'S EMPIRE I, II, III, IV

THE DOPEMAN'S BODYGAURD I II

THE REALEST KILLAZ I II III

THE LAST OF THE OGS I II III

Tranay Adams

THE STREETS ARE CALLING

Duquie Wilson

MARRIED TO A BOSS I II III

By Destiny Skai & Chris Green

KINGZ OF THE GAME I II III IV V VI

Playa Ray

SLAUGHTER GANG I II III

RUTHLESS HEART I II III

By Willie Slaughter

FUK SHYT

By Blakk Diamond

DON'T F#CK WITH MY HEART I II

By Linnea

ADDICTED TO THE DRAMA I II III

IN THE ARM OF HIS BOSS II

By Jamila

YAYO I II III IV

A SHOOTER'S AMBITION I II

BRED IN THE GAME

By S. Allen

TRAP GOD I II III

RICH $AVAGE

MONEY IN THE GRAVE I II

By Martell Troublesome Bolden

FOREVER GANGSTA

GLOCKS ON SATIN SHEETS I II

By Adrian Dulan

TOE TAGZ I II III

LEVELS TO THIS SHYT I II

By Ah'Million

KINGPIN DREAMS I II III
By Paper Boi Rari
CONFESSIONS OF A GANGSTA I II III IV
By Nicholas Lock
I'M NOTHING WITHOUT HIS LOVE
SINS OF A THUG
TO THE THUG I LOVED BEFORE
By Monet Dragun
CAUGHT UP IN THE LIFE I II III
THE STREETS NEVER LET GO
By Robert Baptiste
NEW TO THE GAME I II III
MONEY, MURDER & MEMORIES I II III
By **Malik D. Rice**
LIFE OF A SAVAGE I II III
A GANGSTA'S QUR'AN I II III
MURDA SEASON I II III
GANGLAND CARTEL I II III
CHI'RAQ GANGSTAS I II III
KILLERS ON ELM STREET I II III
JACK BOYZ N DA BRONX I II III
A DOPEBOY'S DREAM I II
By **Romell Tukes**
LOYALTY AIN'T PROMISED I II
By **Keith Williams**
QUIET MONEY I II III
THUG LIFE I II III

EXTENDED CLIP I II

By **Trai'Quan**

THE STREETS MADE ME I II III

By **Larry D. Wright**

THE ULTIMATE SACRIFICE I, II, III, IV, V, VI

KHADIFI

IF YOU CROSS ME ONCE

ANGEL I II

IN THE BLINK OF AN EYE

By **Anthony Fields**

THE LIFE OF A HOOD STAR

By Ca$h & Rashia Wilson

THE STREETS WILL NEVER CLOSE

By K'ajji

CREAM I II

By Yolanda Moore

NIGHTMARES OF A HUSTLA I II III

By King Dream

CONCRETE KILLA I II

VICIOUS LOYALTY

By Kingpen

HARD AND RUTHLESS I II

MOB TOWN 251

THE BILLIONAIRE BENTLEYS

By Von Diesel

GHOST MOB

Stilloan Robinson

MOB TIES I II III IV

By SayNoMore

BODYMORE MURDERLAND I II III

By Delmont Player

FOR THE LOVE OF A BOSS

By C. D. Blue

MOBBED UP I II III IV

THE BRICK MAN

By King Rio

KILLA KOUNTY

By Khufu

MONEY GAME I II

By Smoove Dolla

A GANGSTA'S KARMA

By FLAME

KING OF THE TRENCHES II

by **GHOST & TRANAY ADAMS**

QUEEN OF THE ZOO

By **Black Migo**

BOOKS BY LDP'S CEO, CA$H

TRUST IN NO MAN

TRUST IN NO MAN 2

TRUST IN NO MAN 3

BONDED BY BLOOD

SHORTY GOT A THUG

THUGS CRY

THUGS CRY 2

THUGS CRY 3

TRUST NO BITCH

TRUST NO BITCH 2

TRUST NO BITCH 3

TIL MY CASKET DROPS

RESTRAINING ORDER

RESTRAINING ORDER 2

IN LOVE WITH A CONVICT

LIFE OF A HOOD STAR

Money in the Grave 2

CPSIA information can be obtained
at www.ICGtesting.com
Printed in the USA
LVHW021929240222
711933LV00010B/1137